BEAUTY AND THE WEREWOLF

A SAN FRANCISCO WOLF PACK NOVEL

BEAUTY AND THE WEREWOLF

A SAN FRANCISCO WOLF PACK NOVEL

KRISTIN MILLER

Entangled Publishing, LLC
2614 South Timberline Road
Suite 109
Fort Collins, CO 80525
Visit our website at www.entangledpublishing.com.

Covet is an imprint of Entangled Publishing, LLC.

Edited by Candace Havens
Cover design by Erin Dameron-Hill
Cover photos from 123rf and Shutterstock

Manufactured in the United States of America

First Edition August 2015

To Justin
For making me feel like the most beautiful woman in the world,
every day for the last seventeen years.

For man, as for flower and beast...
the supreme triumph is to be the most vividly, most perfectly
alive.

— D.H. Lawrence

Chapter One

Painting in the middle of the night wasn't all it was cracked up to be.

To the average non-shifter, it might've been the two-hundred-year-old werewolf howling at the full moon that spoiled things. He might've appeared frightening—the ridge of his back arching high as streams of golden moonlight glinted off the sharp points of his canines.

But no.

To Isabelle Connelly, it was the weather kinking her plans.

Gusts of winter wind whipped over the Cliffs of Moher and slammed into Isabelle, freezing her to the bone. She clutched her paintbrush tightly and swiped gently across the canvas to accent the slope of Neil's tail.

"If you don't stop twitching," she said, staring down her furry subject over the top ridge of her clipboard, "I swear to God I'll paint you with a chipmunk tail."

We've been out here for hours, and the weather's only getting worse, he said through the Irish Wolf Pack communication process of mind-speak. His voice, smooth in its lilt, hummed through her head. *I'm freezing my arse off.*

Toughen up, she projected back. *At least you've got your coat to keep you warm.*

Well, she had a trench coat on, but nothing blocked the wind like layers of fur. Isabelle knew firsthand. Being born to werewolf parents meant she could shift at whim—full moon or not. And although the pull of the moon tugged on something in her middle, urging her to shift into a wolf and join Neil, she resisted.

We should go before someone sees us, he said.

We'll be fine. She adjusted the portable LED light illuminating her palette. *The tourists are long gone.*

Even in human form, she could propel her thoughts into Neil's mind. He could block her if the urge struck him, but he'd be stupid to obstruct the mind-speak of the Alpha's only daughter.

Besides, she continued, standing back to admire her work, *I'm almost finished.*

Kinking her neck and narrowing her eyes, Isabelle focused on the dark-haired wolf, his hunched back and striking blue eyes set against the stunning backdrop of shadowed cliff and raging sea. She tapped her brush against the canvas, creating a haze of black fur around his tail.

A few more minutes. She dabbed the brush, whipping the tip to give Neil's tail a stronger emphasis. *The fear of being caught out here is part of the thrill.* She stood back after a final stroke. *Okay. You can give it a look.*

Thank God. Neil bounded away from the rocky ledge of the cliff. He gave a full body shake as he approached her side and set his gaze on the painting. *It's amazing, Isabelle. My mum is going to love this.*

I'm glad, she thought, and swiped her hands on her painting pants. *She's been so kind to me over the years, it's the least I could do.*

Neil's mother had worked in Connelly Castle as one of the serving maids when Isabelle was young. Mary had been the only female figure in Isabelle's life—all 107 years of it. Since Neil was Mary's only son, he'd grown up in the castle, too, and had become more like a brother than a friend.

He looked up at her with wide wolf eyes. *You sure you don't want me showing it to Mr. Connelly?*

"No." Her voice broke the silence of the night. "My dad doesn't want anything to do with my art."

She may've been little Isabelle Connelly to her father, but she was Bella Nolan to the art world. Her paintings of werewolves in majestic settings had been sold worldwide, sometimes for hundreds of thousands of dollars. There weren't many who knew the truth.

But you've got a magic touch with those paintings of yours. You're a rising star in London. He padded his paws around the dirt. *Probably America, too. Wouldn't Mr. Connelly like to know before he—*

"I'm working up the nerve to show him," she interrupted, removing the canvas from the board. "But I want to do it on my terms, and in my own time."

Neil didn't know, but she'd already set in motion the plan to reveal the truth to her disapproving father. She'd spent the last year hunting down her paintings from all over the globe. She'd tracked the auction circuit, noting buyers' addresses, and making them offers they couldn't refuse.

Money wasn't a problem.

Not when time was slipping through her fingers. She didn't have long to show her father what she'd accomplished with her art. He'd been sick for a little more than a year; a rare form of cancer that affected only werewolves had spread from his lungs to his lymph nodes. Wolf pack doctors had given him less than two years to live, though they couldn't know for certain how long he really had left.

Grief trickled into her heart and summoned tears to her eyes as she slipped the canvas into her bag. Even though it'd been a year since her father's diagnosis, the pain stung as strongly as it had the first day.

Her father had told her the sickness was a blessing: every werewolf had to die when its time came, but this way, they could experience every moment as if it were their last. Their days would be lively and bright, heightened by the imminent loss. He'd told her to tie up loose ends. Say what needed to be said before his final breath.

Before he was gone.

But there was still one thing left undone, one thing she couldn't say. More than anything, she wanted her father to see all of her artwork together, in one place, before he closed his eyes and succumbed to the eternal sleep.

Maybe then, when all thirty pieces were together again, he would understand the depth of her passion, the fire in her heart, and the talent in her hand. The world had embraced her paintings, even if they didn't have a clue werewolves existed. Why couldn't her father, the Alpha of their Irish Wolf Pack, embrace them—and her—too?

But you might not have much time left, Neil projected. *My mum says it's getting worse by the day.*

"I know." Fighting back tears, she scrawled her pseudonym on the bottom right hand corner of the picture, the way she always did. Large *B*, illegible "ella." Long, swooping legs of the *N*, scribbly "olan." "I've spent the entire year rounding up my paintings. I'm storing them in Dublin, in a room at the National Gallery of Ireland. I don't have them all yet, but I'm close."

When you're ready, let me know, and I'll have my mum drop this one off, too.

"Thanks, Neil. That means a lot."

Neil huffed in approval as puffs of condensation rose in

front of his face. *How many Bella Nolan pieces are still in the wild?*

"Twelve, I think." She gathered up her painting supplies and tried not to think about how long it would take her to find the last few pieces of art. "Well, thirteen, if you count the first painting I did of my father. But that one is long gone now."

What happened to—

Her phone bleeped from her bag, interrupting him, thank goodness. She didn't want to delve into what happened with her first painting. How could she explain the story, yet hide the pain? Her father had said painting was a waste of time. An Alpha's daughter should spend her days and nights studying tradition and pack policy. How could she express the shame she'd felt when her father flung her precious first piece of art into the hearth?

It hadn't been lit when he'd chucked it, but after she'd left his den crying, she'd heard his order for the fires to be lit. She'd felt the warmth spread through their mansion outside the city. The sharp, shameful burn of disgrace smoldered deep in her heart, even now.

Her phone bleeped again, silencing the thoughts of her father's disapproval. She yanked the cell out of her supply bag and read the text as it flashed over her screen: *Found another Bella Nolan piece in San Francisco:* Werewolf in Venice.

"Thank God." Jolts of elation shot through her. "Finally found you."

Werewolf in Venice had always been one of her favorites. She'd painted it fifteen years ago on her third trip to Italy. She could still remember the fluid lines of the water, the fanciful stone dwellings, and the sleek form of the gray werewolf as it stood proudly in the center of the bridge over Rio di Palazzo.

She read the next text as it popped up: *Up for auction next Saturday, 10:00 a.m. McDougal's Auction House in San Francisco.*

She wouldn't have to mess with a buyer or collector, offer a price, and negotiate until she was blue in the face.

No, this would be easy.

Werewolf in Venice was about to come home.

Deep inside her, something tugged.

Her father had always loved Venice. It was where he took her mum for their final anniversary before her death. She couldn't wait to see her father's face light up when he set his eyes on all her work displayed in one place. In Dublin. Their hometown.

"I hate to cut this short, Neil," Isabelle said, gathering the last of her things. "But I've got a plane to catch to San Francisco."

Sounds like a good time, Neil projected, nudging the bag of brushes closer to her foot. *Just make sure you don't leave your heart there.*

"What does that mean?" She turned to him.

You know, like the song. His big, furry head swung from side to side. *I left my heart, in San…Fran…Cisco.*

"Just so you know, Neil," she said, slinging her bag over her shoulder, "You don't sing any better as a wolf. Still tone-deaf."

He bumped her playfully, and she laughed.

Where will you stay? He rested on his back haunches. *The San Francisco Wolf Pack doesn't welcome us anymore. Not after your father's last visit with the late Mr. MacGrath.*

"I know," she said, thinking about the bad blood between the MacGraths and the Connellys. "But I'm not worried about it. I doubt I'll run into anyone from that family, actually. I'm going to get my painting back, and get home as quickly as possible."

Nothing was going to stop her.

Chapter Two

Saturday morning, as Isabelle strode through the front door of McDougal's in downtown San Francisco, she was handed a pamphlet of the day's artwork. Scanning through the listing, she spotted her piece. The air caught in her throat as she skipped up the marble front steps. She passed large pots crammed with bamboo stalks and towering sculptures of samurai warriors. Folding up the pamphlet, Isabelle shoved it in her purse and strode into the auction room.

The hall was immaculately clean and crowded with people. Her stomach fluttered with happy nerves, and her heart raced in anticipation.

Today was going to be a great day.

After being assigned a paddle, she slid into a seat at the back of the auction hall. Two men brought out each beautifully mastered work. The history of the piece was read, along with a brief summary of which collections it'd been featured in. Whispers spread through the crowd before everyone went quiet and let their paddles do the talking.

"We're going to take a brief intermission before the

next painting, *Werewolf in Venice,*" the auctioneer said, his voice flat. But it wasn't the tone of his voice that had Isabelle searching the features of the old man's face. It was the Irish brogue. "Everyone, take ten."

He marched down the center aisle and slid into the seat next to her as if he'd planned the intermission for the very reason.

"You look at me strange, Isabelle, as if you don't recognize me. I'm Colin O'Hare." He extended his hand. "It's been years since I've rested my hat in Dublin, but I didn't think my beard had gone *that* gray."

Recognition hit her, and she gasped.

Colin had been a member of their pack for two hundred years before venturing out on his own. Rumors hit Dublin that he'd gone to California, but no one had said anything about his work in the auction circuit.

"Oh my gosh, I'm so sorry I didn't recognize you." She shook his hand. It was warm and calloused, like worn leather. "I didn't know you worked for McDougal's." Might've made her task of tracking down her lost art an easier one. "How've you been?"

"Well, thank you." He leaned in close and whispered, "How's your father holdin' up?"

She sighed as despair weighed heavy on her shoulders. "Good as can be, I guess. Did you hear he's fighting cancer?"

"Aye." Colin nodded, and the lights shone off the bald patch on the top of his head. "Let me tell you, lass, if any man can win that battle, it's Gerard Connelly. I've never met a man with so much fire." He tapped her chin gently, as a father would do to a child. "That fire is in you as well."

Something inside her softened, and she ached to change the subject before she broke completely. "I'm here to bid on *Werewolf in Venice,*" she said as nonchalantly as she could. "I hear it's beautiful."

"You're a fan of Bella Nolan, are ya?"

She nodded slowly and averted her gaze to the seat back in front of her. "I suppose you could say I am."

"That piece is mighty fine. Sold last year in London for three and a quarter."

She swelled with pride, but kept the emotion on lockdown. Colin didn't have a clue she was the artist. Or, rather, if he did, he hadn't let on.

She'd probably have to pay more than four hundred thousand to get it back. Between the earnings from her work and the savings in the Connelly vault, she could afford a solid bid, thank goodness.

"I'd love to sit an' chat with you, dear, but I've got to be gettin' back." He took her hand, flipped it over, and kissed her knuckles. "It was lovely to see you. Send my love to your father, and the rest of the pack."

Her heart warmed. "I will."

As he returned to the podium at the front, Isabelle sensed someone watching her. She scanned the room, over unfamiliar faces from one side and back again. Sniffing softly, she used her heightened sense of smell to detect anything out of the ordinary. She could pick up extreme emotions: fury and fear, love and happiness. Happiness—a sweet and rosy scent— tingled her nose, masking every other scent in the room.

Nothing out of the ordinary.

"The next piece is *Werewolf in Venice* by Bella Nolan," Colin announced as the piece was escorted to the stage. "It's a stunning piece of Gothic realism."

He detailed every gallery her art had been featured in, every collection where it'd been shown over the last few years. Awareness heated Isabelle's cheeks and made the rest of his words fuzzy in her ears. It always happened this way when someone spoke fondly of her work.

"Let's start the bidding at two hundred thousand."

She flushed hot as a paddle went up, directly across the aisle from her.

Good God, that man—scratch that...she sniffed and picked up a familiar scent—that *werewolf*, was gorgeous. Midnight black hair cut close to his head on the sides and longer on top. Big brown eyes. Strong nose. A layer of stubble covering his wide jaw. Black suit and tie. One foot kicked up and resting over the opposite leg.

He gave off a vibe of dominance mixed with cool and composed nobleness.

He lifted his paddle again as the bid jumped to two hundred fifty thousand. He didn't hesitate. Not once. Not even when the price rose to five and a quarter.

Flattery struck her, but she quickly dismissed it. No matter how good it felt knowing the total hottie wanted to have her picture, she couldn't—*wouldn't*—let it go.

"Six hundred thousand to Mr. MacGrath," Colin said. "Any other bids?"

Isabelle's gaze snapped to the Greek god.

MacGrath?

Oh, she had his number now.

He may've been sexy as hell, but he was a snake. Evil to the core. Just like every other MacGrath in their nasty family line.

She lifted her chin defiantly and raised her paddle.

· · ·

Jack refused to be outbid. He'd been waiting for *Werewolf in Venice* to come up for auction again so he could acquire it and add it to his collection of Bella Nolan work.

He was inexplicably drawn to Nolan's paintings. They were breathtaking. She brilliantly weaved the majestic form of the werewolf into the natural cityscape behind it. It was the stroke of her brush over the wolves in the painting—gentle and soft—against the gritty textures in the background that had captivated him.

When he studied Nolan's artwork, a rush of something hot streaked through him. It was akin to a surge of adrenaline. He couldn't explain the feeling, and had given up trying to figure it out.

He had eleven Bella Nolan paintings.

Werewolf in Venice would make twelve.

And he wasn't about to be outbid by the tiny little pixie sitting in the row across from him. She had dark hair that dropped past her shoulders and curled up at the ends. Bright green eyes lined with thick lashes. Freckles covering her plump cheeks. She was a werewolf—he could tell by the sweet and spicy smell of her—but she wasn't from the San Francisco Wolf Pack.

He would've run into her by now, and he never forgot a face.

The pixie wore a thick black scarf, black heels, and a black dress that revealed the porcelain-smooth length of her legs when she crossed them. Judging from her attire, she was either headed to a funeral after the auction or stuck in a permanent state of melancholy. Or maybe she simply thought the monochromatic color would make her incognito.

Yeah, no way. With legs like that, anonymity was impossible.

As the bid tiptoed higher, reaching six hundred fifteen thousand, Jack raised his paddle with a flick of his wrist. He couldn't care less about the money spent. He'd accumulated an estate worth billons, but even if he hadn't, he'd go in debt to hang *Werewolf in Venice* on his walls.

Besides, he couldn't take his billions with him when he died, so he might as well spend his money on something he could enjoy in his final days.

Seeing as how he was a 320-year-old werewolf who'd yet to find his Luminary—his one and only fated mate—he was weakening. Werewolves could only live about three hundred years without going through the bonding process with their Luminary. With every year that passed by, he was pushing the envelope.

He'd searched tirelessly for his mate. Scoured wolf packs throughout the country, and had come up empty-handed. Luminaries could feel the spark of connection at first touch.

He'd failed. End of discussion. End of his life.

A shaky breath ripped from his lungs.

Just then, he picked up something else in the pixie's scent. Hints of something rich and creamy. It smelled almost like—no, it couldn't possibly be—*Guinness*? Smooth and full. Bittersweet underneath. Had she drunk the beer recently? Was it still on her breath?

He couldn't tell.

The pixie lifted her chin—a slight move, but he caught it—and raised her paddle.

Guess she was a Bella Nolan fan, too.

Without thinking twice, he rebutted.

She craned her neck to the side and glared at him, kinking one eyebrow. It was clear that she was trying to give him attitude, but she looked downright adorable. Like a puppy gearing up for battle against a more formidable dog. He couldn't help but smile.

Sweetheart, I'm 320 years old. I've met and outbid enthusiastic bidders like you before.

But you've never met me.

Her thoughts struck him like a hammer to the temples. He hadn't meant to project his thoughts, or for her to hear them. But now that she'd responded, he couldn't get the sweet sound of her voice out of his head. Her tone was light and airy, like the winter wind, carrying a soft accent.

He couldn't place it. English? Irish? Definitely European.

With a huff, the pixie redirected her attention to the front. And raised the bid again.

I can do this all day. Her lips twitched in irritation as her words pulsed through his mind. *You might as well go home now. It'll save you some embarrassment.*

Exhilaration fired through his veins.

There was only one thing he loved more than a challenge: a tantalizing game of cat-and-mouse.

Keeping his eye on her, Jack bid until the price reached seven hundred fifty thousand and the room erupted in excited whispers. Pixie fidgeted in her seat, shifting her weight from one hip to the other.

Don't overextend yourself, he projected.

Don't worry about me. She waved her paddle. *Worry about what your friends in the auction circuit are going to think when you're outbid and lose this painting.*

He bid again. Without hearing the next price.

She matched him.

A smirk curled the corner of his lips as he met her eyes. Fiery determination burned in those emerald depths. Her eyes stunned him, twinkling bright and holding him captive. But not enough to miss the price of the painting rise near a million.

He winked. And then lifted the paddle slowly.

She fumed, her nostrils pushing out slightly, her lips tightening in agitation.

As the room quieted, Jack's heart raced. Time slowed. Something hot, like molten lava, flooded through his body, making his arms and legs weak. It was the same reaction he had when he pushed the limit and cheated death.

He'd become intimately familiar with the feeling.

Since adrenaline rushes were the only way he was staying alive, he'd had to find new and interesting ways to keep the blood hammering through his veins. For the past twenty years, he'd been living on borrowed time, jumping from one heart-pounding adventure to another.

Although he couldn't explain it, the pixie sitting across from him was giving him a rush. It was new, interesting, and *definitely* heart-pounding.

He didn't want to let *Werewolf in Venice* slip through his fingers, but what if he *let her* outbid him? It'd be a loss to his collection, sure, but if he took home the painting, the pixie would be angry and embarrassed. Unforgiving. If he let her win, however, he could congratulate her. Strike up conversation. Invite her to dinner where they'd talk about their mutual love of Nolan's work. And then, when dessert came to the table, he'd escort her back to his place.

He'd gladly lose the painting to keep the adrenaline pumping through his veins the way it was now.

A tiny *bleep* sounded from her direction. Dropping her paddle into her lap, she fished her cell phone out of her purse and checked the screen. If Jack wasn't mistaken, the color drained from her cheeks. She blinked quickly, her lips parting in disbelief. Or was it sadness…?

"Sold," the auctioneer declared from the front, "to Mr. Jack MacGrath for one million dollars."

Victory.

The pixie flipped her gaze to the front and then to him. Alarm flickered in her eyes before she stared at her phone once more.

Congratulations on your win, she projected, sliding out into the aisle. *It's too bad the piece didn't go to someone who'd truly appreciate it. Good day.*

What the hell did she know about him or the art he appreciated?

He watched his painting being escorted to the back and then followed the pixie into the foyer.

She was already gone.

He'd just purchased *Werewolf in Venice* to add to his collection—the only reason he'd come to McDougal's today—yet he couldn't shake the feeling that he'd left something unfinished. Hairs on the back of his neck stood on end. The only way to get rid of the prickly sensation, he'd learned, was to jump into the day's hectic schedule. Check things off his list. One by one. He didn't even know the pixie's name, so he'd never see her again. Putting her behind him wasn't going to be a problem.

That's exactly what he'd do: completely forget about her.

Right after he hit up Johnny Foley's Irish Pub and quenched his thirst for a Guinness.

Chapter Three

Early the next morning, Isabelle took the address Colin had reluctantly given her and drove her rented Camry into Monterey Heights. She hadn't expected a guy like Jack MacGrath—a recluse, from what she'd heard—to live in a city as booming as San Francisco.

As she approached a large, grassy lot surrounded by a high iron fence, she knew she'd found the right place. She couldn't see much of the house from the street, but it appeared to be three stories. Mission-like architecture. Clean landscaping.

Isabelle put the Camry in park in front of the gated entrance to the mansion and rolled down the window. Determined not to let *Werewolf in Venice* go, she punched the red speaker button.

"I'm here to see Jack MacGrath," she said.

A gentleman on the other end of the line asked a question. An annoying buzz over the line muddled his words.

She slumped into the seat and sighed.

Never in a million years would she have thought she'd be here.

Through the years, Isabelle's father had told her about how the MacGrath family had made their fortune. They'd journeyed from Europe in the 1700s, settled in San Francisco, and started a foreign currency trading brokerage to assist other immigrating werewolves. Rather than being helpful—or God forbid, *honest*—they pilfered clients' accounts, stocking away millions while their foreign werewolf "brothers" floundered. Through the years, the MacGrath family was rumored to be involved in investment fraud and corporate deceit, leaving empty bank accounts in their wake.

Getting a leg up by stepping on others was sickening.

Most recently, the MacGraths were believed to be involved in a two-hundred-million-dollar art heist. A painting by Vincent van Gogh—black and white poppy flowers, if she remembered the story right—had been stolen in broad daylight from a museum in Switzerland. Her father had said that the werewolves hidden in the Switzerland government believed a MacGrath was involved.

Out of all of his thieving family members, Jack was the one involved in the auction circuit.

He was also a recluse, keeping people at a distance... probably so no one could get close enough to discover the truth about his involvement in the heist and turn him in. She didn't need to be a detective to know he was behind the whole thing.

He was a MacGrath by name and blood: guilty until proven innocent.

"Tell Mr. MacGrath that Isabelle Connelly is here to see him." She spoke loudly into the intercom. "I'd like to make an offer on his newest piece of acquired art: *Werewolf in Venice*."

Silence followed after a deafeningly loud crackling sound.

Five minutes dragged by. She tapped her fingers on the steering wheel and refused to move. Stared at the intricate ironwork on the gate.

"I'm not leaving," she mumbled to herself. "Not until I get my painting."

Nothing else mattered.

Billionaire or not, everything had a price.

She'd simply have to make him an offer he couldn't refuse. Hell if she knew what that was, though.

Without warning, the gates let out a groan, startling her. She jumped in her seat and watched them open slowly, revealing a winding stone-paved driveway. She put the Camry in gear and drove toward a towering fountain erected in the middle of the driveway.

But the closer she got to the fountain, the slower she drove.

She gawked, mouth hanging open in disbelief.

Good God, the fountain was hideously phallic. Like a giant penis standing ramrod-straight in the middle of a gravel bed. Water bubbled up from the tip, making her throw up a little in her mouth.

Craning her neck around, Isabelle shook her head and scoffed.

It was a disgustingly perfect fountain for a guy like Jack MacGrath.

As she turned, veering away from the fountain—out of pure instinct—she realized she was now parked facing the stairs to his mansion. And took up the width of the driveway, hood to rear end.

Damn it.

She should've just parked next to the damn thing.

Glancing in the rearview mirror, she reversed carefully. As she inched closer to the penis monolith, the unmistakable *whop-whop-whop* of a helicopter sounded in the distance. The racket increased.

Was a helicopter landing on the damn house?

She bent, craning to look beneath the doorframe. She

searched the sky. One way, and then the other.

There it was.

A freaking helicopter swooped over his house, making a low dive over her car.

She squealed, ducking low in her seat.

The thunderous *flac-flac-flac* of the blades drowned out everything—the rumble of the Camry's engine and the drumming of her own heart—as it dropped out of the sky and hovered above the large lawn on the opposite end of the estate. The chopper was massive. Menacing. A door on the side slid open. A rope was flung out, hitting the grass.

What the hell?

With a jolt, the tires of her car ran over something crackly. Her car bumbled. Shook. And then backed into something solid.

"Oh, shit!" Isabelle gripped the wheel tight and slammed on the brakes. Whipping around, she glared out the back window...and caught the breath in her throat. She must've been inching back without realizing it. She'd rear-ended the giant penis. It wobbled, shook. The tip seemed loose, teetering on the thick base. "No, no, no, don't—"

And then it fell. Dropped right to the ground with a *thud*.

Cue mortification.

Blood heated her cheeks. "Perfect."

Maybe she could get out of there so she wouldn't have to see Jack MacGrath face-to-face. She could get his email from Colin. Send him a note saying she was the one responsible for the fountain. He could bill her. She'd replace his disgusting sculpture.

As she put the car in gear and eased away from the fountain, Jack MacGrath leaped out of the helicopter, the rope in his grasp.

Isabelle froze, gawking through the side window.

He rappelled to the ground effortlessly, stalling three

times before hitting grass. He gave a salute to the pilot and watched as the chopper flew over the house and out of sight.

She would've thought he was practicing some sort of military procedure...except he wore loose-fitting jeans, a black T-shirt pulled taut over his chest, and a black-and-white pair of Converse.

The whole thing was surreal.

They were in the *city* for crying out loud. Not a freaking army base.

He stalked closer. Nerves spiraled through her. It was now or never. She could jet out of here and send her apologies over Hotmail or she could face him.

She'd never been one to walk away from a confrontation.

She wouldn't start now.

Steeling herself for battle, Isabelle turned off her car and stepped out.

"Mr. MacGrath, I'm Isabelle Connelly. We met yesterday at the auction house." Her stomach clenched when she looked into his warm caramel-brown eyes. "I came by to talk to you, but I'm afraid I may have destroyed your fountain." Geez, the words really rattled out of her when she was nervous. "I'll replace it. I insist."

Crease lines formed on his forehead as he frowned. And then he followed her gaze to the tip of the sculpture rolling around in the gravel bed.

"What happened?" he asked, crouching down to pick it up.

She leaned against the trunk to steady herself. "I was distracted by the damn helicopter. I didn't expect it to come swooping out of the sky like that. And then you— What were you doing, anyway? Are you in the army?"

"Not anymore."

"Then why—"

"I don't like heights." He said it simply. As if his answer

made all the sense in the world. It didn't. "Rappelling like that is a wild ride. My buddy still flies and offered to take me up."

"You didn't look afraid of heights to me."

No, he was cool and confident as if he'd performed maneuvers like that a thousand times before. Strong…and *sexy*.

"I didn't say I was afraid. I said I don't *like* heights. Makes for a crazy rush." He flung the head of the penis to the grass behind him and then eyed her carefully. "That's all that matters anymore."

So he didn't like rappelling from helicopters, yet did it anyway…for the adrenaline rush? *Interesting*.

"I'm sorry about that," she said, nudging her chin at the decapitated shaft. "I'll give you my email address before I leave and you can send me the bill."

"I'll take the address, but forget about the bill." The corners of his full lips turned up at the corners. "I always hated this fountain. It came with the house and I simply haven't bothered to rip it out. You want to back into it again? Knock it over completely?"

He hated the fountain?

Okay, okay, so he might've dropped down a few clicks on her douche-meter.

Still a MacGrath, she reminded herself. Just because he didn't bow down to a cement penis in his driveway didn't mean he was made of gold.

"As much as I'd love to plow into the ugly thing again, I can't." She reached behind her and patted the trunk of the car. "It's a rental, and I fear I've already dinged it."

Without warning, he approached the back of the Camry and dropped to bended knee. She retreated a few steps, though she couldn't tear her eyes away from him. He ghosted his fingers over the curves of the bumper, over the paint, searching for damage. Something in her stomach tugged. She'd been jealous of many things in her life: gorgeous blondes, and women who could eat whatever they wanted without getting fat, to name a couple. But she'd never, not once, been jealous of a car.

How ridiculous.

Still…

The way he touched it, with the softest of strokes, made her swoon inside. She'd had many lovers in her lifetime, but she'd never been touched gently that way. As if she were made of glass. As if she could break under a caress.

"Might be a little scratch right here," he said, his voice rich and husky, "but it isn't too noticeable."

"Good thing that penis of yours was so fragile." She couldn't help but giggle as the words tumbled out. "One nudge and it toppled right over."

Rather than laugh with her, he stood and met her gaze. "Believe me, love, *it* doesn't topple over that easily."

As her laugh faded away, a quiver shook her to the core.

• • •

It must've been the adrenaline lingering in his veins.

Had to be.

It couldn't be this woman and her infectious laugh that had a warm rush tingling through him.

He'd tried to put Isabelle behind him last night, but she'd tortured him. She was in every dream—her button nose and sparkling green eyes, her radiant smile and delicious scent. He couldn't escape her. So he'd made plans to head out with one of his old army buddies first thing in the morning.

At this point, he needed adrenaline rushes morning and night to keep his ticker going strong. At least that's what the wolf pack medicine man had said. He'd told him to keep his adrenaline levels high. Always. But the rushes were harder and harder to achieve as his body adapted to the exhilaration. At first, he could stand near the edge of his roof to get the spike in his blood; heights truly did make him uncomfortable. He hadn't lied to her. But now, he had to jump out of planes or helicopters, or BASE jump off skyscrapers.

Anything to stay alive another day.

Sadly, his hands had begun to shake two weeks ago—another sign of his mortality, or so he'd been told. Things were going to get worse. Shakes would turn to long-lasting tremors, and then to seizures. Soon after that, his heart would stop and none of this would mean anything anymore.

"So you're visiting from Ireland?" he asked.

She planted her hands on her hips. "What, I don't pass for an American?"

"You definitely sound American—your accent is a muddled blend of everything—so it'd be easy for others to think you're from here. But I catch your Irish lilt coming through every now and again. I take it that comes from being well-traveled?"

"It does." Her expression pinched in confusion. "I've been around the world a few times over, and I lived on the East Coast back in the twenties. There have been a few times, in Dublin, when non-shifters took me for an American. They said it was the way I talked." She smirked. "I must be rude and think the world owes me something."

"No, it's because of the words you choose."

He'd traveled the world, too. His family had been some of the first to settle in America from England, and a few of them hadn't conducted business with an honorable hand. To escape the shame of the family name, Jack had spent over a hundred years traveling. Carving out his name in the world, apart from the reputation his ancestors had given him.

But he didn't want to talk about them. "What can I do for you, Isabelle?"

"I'm here to make you an offer on *Werewolf in Venice.*"

He folded his arms over his chest. "Well, let's hear it."

Deep breath. "I'll double what you paid at auction."

He couldn't force out a laugh, though he should've. "Not happening, Ms. Connelly. You might as well return the car and head back to wherever it was you came from."

"But I'm not finished talking about the painting." She seemed to fume, her nostrils pushing out a bit. "It's beautiful, but you paid too much out the gate. Good thing for you I showed up to make a generous offer. Take the money and invest in another painting. By another artist, if you prefer."

"Nothing compares to a Bella Nolan painting."

Her supple lips parted, and then clamped shut. "I'm sure Bella Nolan is flattered, wherever she is. But I'd be paying you more than the painting is worth. You could take the money and—"

"You're not getting it. I don't want the money. Not double, or triple." Damn, he relished the back-and-forth between them. Fiery impulses were really shooting through his veins now. He pointed to the mansion towering behind her. "I have everything I could ever need, and I can't take it with me when I'm buried six feet under." He swallowed down the bile rising in the back of his throat. "Why would I want more useless green paper?"

Shifting her weight from one foot to the other, Isabelle worried her bottom lip between her teeth. The painting must've been more important to her than she was letting on.

"Listen, Mr. MacGrath…"

The way she said his name had his blood boiling hot.

"…the painting is important to me. I wouldn't be here if it wasn't. If you don't want the money, that's fine, but everything has a price and I'm willing to pay just about anything."

Sparks of curiosity went off like fireworks in his mind. *Anything, huh?*

As a mischievous smile pulled at the corners of his mouth, his hands began to tremble Uncrossing his arms, he glanced down at his palms. They quivered and shook.

This can't be happening.

Not so soon after the chopper ride. The shakes should've stayed away much longer. Isabelle may've been willing to give anything to have the painting, but she couldn't give him the one thing he needed most: more time.

No one could give him that.

He had to find a way to hold on.

"The painting's not for sale," he bit out. "But it was great seeing you again."

She swiped her tongue over her teeth, and drew her bottom lip into her mouth again. Damn, if her lips weren't the most erotic thing he'd ever seen in his life.

"There has to be something—my father is the Alpha of the Irish Wolf Pack and I'm sure there's something that can be done—"

Frustration roared through him. "There's nothing."

"The rumors about your family are true." She narrowed her eyes at him. "You're conniving and shrewd, just as I thought you'd be."

"I have a few family members who fit the mold you've described," he said as his lips pulled into a frown, "but that's not me."

"After this encounter, I don't wish to find out if that's true. Good day," she said, extending her hand. "I pray it's the last we meet."

He may've been short with her about the painting, but he didn't wish the same. He wouldn't mind seeing her again. Under different circumstances, of course.

Even though his arm trembled, he clutched her hand and shook. Without warning, electric currents zinged through him, jagged and hot. Straight through his palm and up his arm.

Soul-searing pain splintered into his shoulder and radiated through his chest. The urge to haul her into his arms hit him like a sledgehammer to the temples. The wolf part of him wanted to claim Isabelle as his own, right here and right now, even though he didn't know a damned thing about her. It was irrational, yet the impulses felt as natural as breathing. As sure as the blood hammering through his veins, Isabelle Connelly was *his*. With a jolt, he took back his hand and rubbed it on his jeans.

Nodding good-bye, she strode toward the driver's door of her car.

But wait—hadn't she felt what he had?

Two seconds ago, he'd been facing certain death. He could've keeled over in months, days, or minutes. Hell, he could've died right at her feet. But now, if they bonded as werewolf mates, he had another seven hundred years ahead of him.

He'd given up hope of ever finding her and feeling the connection. His fated mate.

And now here she was—his *Luminary*—right in his grasp.

"Wait." He was at her door in two sure strides. "You can't go."

"Oh, I can and I will." She yanked the door open and slid inside. "Watch me."

He clutched the door and held it apart from the car's frame. Kneeling, he blocked the gap so she couldn't close the door on him.

"How can you feel that and just leave?"

Staring as if he were crazy, Isabelle brought the car to life. "Feel what? Anger? Resentment? Disappointment that I traveled all that way from Ireland to make an offer to the most unreasonable MacGrath in the family line?"

His stomach soured and then knotted into a rotten pit.

She hadn't felt the spark. If she had, she wouldn't have

been talking this way.

The Luminary spark was different for every wolf. Based on the pack dynamic, position in the pack, or the age of the partner, each werewolf would feel something unique. He'd been so eager to find his mate, he'd never considered the fact that she might not feel the spark the same way he had.

"The Luminary spark." The words burned his tongue. "You're my fated mate."

"Ha!" She laughed the word. "I thought you were crazy when you jumped out of a perfectly safe helicopter, but now…" Shaking her head, she laughed and laughed. And put the car in drive. "You're certifiable."

"But the zing. The electricity when we touched." He stared, waiting for some kind of recognition in her eyes. *Nothing*. "You didn't feel it?"

She pursed her lips. "If you don't get out of the way, Jack MacGrath, I might run you over and leave two dickheads lying on your driveway."

He couldn't let her slip through his fingers. Not now.

She couldn't go back to Ireland.

As she hit the gas, jerking the car door from his grasp, he stood and hollered, "I'll give you the painting."

Brake lights.

This time, when she reversed, he jumped out of the way. Rolling down the window, Isabelle stuck out her elbow and glared. "What do you want?"

Think fast. Think clear.

"I donated a painting to the de Young museum for its exhibit tonight. They've invited me to attend as an honored guest. If you'll be my date, *Werewolf in Venice* will be yours."

It was a small price to pay to add hundreds of years to his life.

"You'll give it to me…just like that." She squinted, disbelieving. "If I go out with you. Yet two million dollars wouldn't cut it?"

"There are some things you can't put a price on." He nodded. Only once. "You can even meet me there, if you'd like. It's black tie. Eight o'clock."

She didn't say a word. But as she pulled out of his driveway and slowed around the corner, he knew he'd see her again.

It was all he needed.

It was everything.

Chapter Four

Make it through the night, get the painting, go home.

Repeating the plan to herself didn't ease her nerves. Parked in a garage in the heart of Golden Gate Park, Isabelle checked her reflection in the mirror for the tenth time. Her hair was in the in-between stage, where it looked too plain if she left it down, but couldn't pull it up without strands falling out. She'd settled for a low updo with tons of bobby pins, and minimal makeup. Her dress was classic. Black silk, down to her ankles, with a slit up the front.

This wasn't really a date, after all, so why bother getting fancy?

It didn't matter what Jack *thought* he felt. There was no spark in his touch. Nothing that would make her even think for one second that he was her Luminary.

Imagine that. A MacGrath and a Connelly. Fated mates.

Scoffing out loud, she adjusted the top of her dress. Her father would freak if he found out what Jack had said. Even thinking about the pairing would make him go ballistic. He'd probably put out a bounty on Jack's head.

Surprisingly, the idea wasn't *entirely* grotesque. He *was* easy on the eyes. But he was also absolutely, undeniably annoying. He wouldn't even *consider* selling her the painting until she was halfway out of his drive.

At least Jack hadn't been as bad as she'd expected. As bad as her father had made a MacGrath out to be. She didn't like to judge people before she knew them, but he'd pummeled into her brain, for years on end, that the family was full of terrible, deceitful people.

She had yet to see that side of Jack, but still…a part of her was waiting for her father's words to ring true.

Lifting the front of the dress she'd bought a few hours before, Isabelle strode up the steps toward the de Young. She nodded to the men in tuxedos who flanked the doors of the museum and swept inside. The place was bursting with life. From paintings illuminated on the walls to classical music wafting from the speakers to sculptures in the corners, everything was vibrant. Even the people. Men dressed in tuxedos and women glammed-up in formal gowns filled the space, mingling and laughing and happily clinking glasses.

Despite the festive atmosphere, Isabelle's shoulders felt tight. Hell, every muscle in her body was on edge. She'd have to bite her tongue for a few hours. Remember not to tell Jack how little her pack thought of his family and the way they did business.

"I need liquid courage," she mumbled, and sauntered toward the bar.

On her way, a server holding a platter of hors d'oeuvres passed in front of her. Looked like snapper crudo with chile, steak lettuce cups, and bites of sesame chicken on sticks.

Scrumptious.

Stomach growling fiercely, Isabelle spun in front of the waiter and snatched a handful of each. *God,* she'd been so preoccupied with dress shopping for tonight, she'd forgotten to eat.

As she shoved the snapper in her mouth and headed for the bar, someone tapped her on the shoulder. She whipped around, shifted the food to her cheek, and bit back a gasp. From his musky, masculine scent to his ruggedly strong jawline to his sultry brown eyes, Jack MacGrath was a vision of sex appeal.

"Looking for me?" he asked.

Choking down the fish, she swiped the back of her hand over her mouth to clear away the crumbs. "No, but I've got a throat on me."

He chuckled, eyeing her neck. "I'm sorry, what?"

"I'm thirsty." She wasn't back at home, drinking with Neil. She'd do well to remember it. "Anyway, what are you drinking?"

"Scotch on the rocks is my poison." He held up a whiskey tumbler full of ice and very little amber liquid. "I was going to ask what yours was, but I see now it's one-bite hors d'oeuvres."

Oh, isn't this grand? I'm a hungry, hungry hippo.

"I don't know what you're talking about." Hiding her hands behind her, Isabelle quickly chucked the rest of the appetizers she'd fisted.

From the direction of the flying food, a woman squealed in shock. Or maybe disgust. She couldn't tell unless she turned to see, and she was most definitely not going to make eye contact and admit fault.

Damn it, what were the chances she'd actually *hit* someone?

"Come on," Isabelle said, snatching Jack by the sleeve of his coat. She jerked him toward the bar. "Think the bar has the black stuff?"

If he knew that she'd just chucked a bunch of bite-sized meat at an unsuspecting guest, he didn't let on. Thank goodness for small victories.

"Black stuff?" He kicked his foot up on a barstool. "You mean tar?"

"No, I mean Guinness."

He winked. "I know what you meant, but some would think those two were one and the same. A Guinness for the beautiful lady," he called to the bartender, and then set his almond-shaped eyes on her. "Anything else?"

"My painting." Smiling smugly, she propped her elbow on the bar. "Since you're offering."

He smiled, but only one corner of his lips quirked, and it was sexy as hell. "We'll get to that."

"I figured, but it was worth a shot."

"Of course it was. Come on," he said, sliding her drink from the bar and handing it to her. "I want to show you something. A taste of home, perhaps."

She followed him reluctantly, merging into the crowd and zigzagging toward an area with a sign that read NATIONAL GALLERIES OF SCOTLAND. He hesitated as she passed through a marble archway, and ghosted a hand over the small of her back. Even though he didn't touch her, she chilled, her skin going tingly all over.

Had they walked under a vent?

They entered the Scottish gallery, and knots of tension loosened in her shoulders. Her arms dropped to her sides.

"Wow, this is grand." She filled her lungs and let out a deep, relaxed sigh. "Really grand."

This was the type of experience she wanted her father to have with her work before he died. He should feel enraptured by the art. As if it were a part of his soul. That's the way she felt when she painted, and why she felt connected to every single piece.

"How long will you be staying in San Francisco?" Jack asked from behind her.

Completely enthralled, she paused in front of a nature

painting by Paul Cézanne. "I'm not sure, but I'm anxious to get back."

"What's the hurry?"

If she wasn't mistaken, he sounded genuinely disappointed. But MacGraths didn't *feel* anything. Ever.

"I miss home." While that was true, there was more to it than that. She wanted to spend every last second with her father, before there weren't any seconds left. Her stomach clenched into a knot as dread seeped in. "I have family waiting for me."

Jack stood beside her as she kinked her head to the side to analyze a painting of a man ice-skating on Duddingston Loch circa 1795. It was a masterpiece. Painting perfection. It'd been created "en plein air" too, if she had to guess by the wisps of light in its layers.

"Have you enjoyed your time in the city?" he asked, his voice tight.

"I find it hard to believe that you bargained tonight for the painting, yet you want to spend our time talking about how much I like the city or how long I'm staying. Is that really why you wanted me here?" She tipped back her drink. "Because I think there's more to it, and it's about time you let me in on the secret."

He leaned in close, and she couldn't help but inhale a generous helping of his masculine scent. He smelled divinely fresh, like amber and sandalwood. An intoxicating combination that had her stunned.

"Oh, I've got secrets," he whispered against her ear. "But this isn't one. Is it so hard to believe that I simply craved your company?"

Good God, her earlobes shivered. Was that even possible?

The thought of this gorgeous man craving *anything* had her mouth watering. Words evaporated from her brain, which didn't happen very often, if ever. Despite herself, she relaxed.

Probably had something to do with that smooth-as-silk voice.

"That's your big secret?" she asked, stepping up to the next painting. "You wanted to spend time with me and chitchat?"

"Sure." He followed her, a constant presence at her side. But he wasn't pushy. Oh no. He glided over the floor a few feet behind her, his free hand in his pocket, the tuxedo coat stretched taut over his impossibly broad shoulders. And damn if those pants didn't pitch over his obviously impressive groin. "Have you done anything fun since you've been in the city?"

Oh, there were a few *fun* things she was thinking about doing at the moment. Enjoyable, naughty things that made her girly bits tingle.

"I'm sorry, what?"

He smirked, as if he had caught her staring at his package. "What have you been doing to occupy your time?"

Keep your eyes up. "I haven't been here long enough to see as much as I would've liked. I flew in right before the auction."

"And you're already eager to return?"

She nodded.

"Why not stay a few days?" His dark eyes glimmered with something devious. "You can see the city while you're here and experience all you can. And let me tell you, hotels are so impersonal. You'd be better off seeing the city from a local's point of view. If you want, you're welcome to crash at my place."

Oh yeah, baby.

No—*wait.*

She was supposed to hate him, wasn't she? He was a MacGrath, for crying out loud. How easily he could make her forget…

"You can waggle your eyebrows all you want, Jack, but I wouldn't go home with you if you had a collection of *ten* Bella

Nolan paintings."

He grinned, as if he hid the most delectable secret. "Actually, I—"

Glasses clinked from the main room, interrupting him. When she met his eyes once more, the dark twinkle in them had vanished. Museum patrons mumbled low, their whispers melting together into an incomprehensible wave of conversation.

"We should see what that's about," she said, watching the crowd form near a large painting on the back wall. "They're starting some sort of speech."

"It's nothing interesting, believe me. Besides, we haven't seen all the artwork in here." Jack brushed by, bumping into her with his shoulder. Gooseflesh pebbled over her arm. "Look at this one."

She was still trying to get rid of the chill spreading through her chest when Jack stopped in front of an oil panting of Niagara Falls.

"I'm blown away by the whole process," he said, "How an artist can take a blank canvas and turn it into a masterpiece. I don't know anything about painting, though artwork like this has always fascinated me."

Isabelle tore her eyes away from the main group and approached his side. "Maybe you should pick up a brush and give it a go. If you're so intrigued by it."

"It's not about the process, so to speak, but the people behind the art. You can almost sense what the artist was feeling when he painted this." Turning slowly, he stared her down with those smoky-brown eyes. And just like that, she was warm again. "I like to collect things by artists I feel connected to. Art, sculptures, valuable books, anything that I can add to my private gallery."

"Sounds like you've got quite the collection," she said, traipsing around the hall. She could feel his gaze boring into her back as she turned away. "But you're focused on acquiring, rather than appreciating. There's a huge difference."

"I disagree. Acquiring *is* appreciating. If I spend a million and a quarter on a piece, it has more value to me than one I paid three hundred thousand for."

She spun and stared. "So the inherent value of something is based on the retail price?"

"Of course." He nodded. "Which piece in this museum gets the most attention? The one in the far corner, or the one in the center in the glass case? The one purchased for fifty thousand, or the one the museum newly acquired for half a million?"

A little piece of her died at the thought of someone buying her paintings solely based on the monetary value.

"We're going to have to agree to disagree," she said plainly.

Jack followed her trek to each of the paintings. A silent companion. She kept her distance from him and was careful not to brush him accidently. Werewolves usually ran hot, their temperatures a bit higher than non-shifters, but when she touched him, an odd chill seeped into her bones.

Finishing her Guinness, Isabelle stopped in front of a family painting. Oil on canvas from the early 1800s. The father in the piece had the little girl on his knee. She held out a golden-yellow rayed flower and smiled brightly. Proudly. Her father beamed, his arms wrapped around his daughter as he gazed into her eyes. The little girl's happiness and her father's love had been captured for eternity.

It was the kind of dynamic she'd envisioned when she'd shown her father her very first painting. She'd wanted him to wrap her in his arms. Tell her how proud he was of her. Encourage her to paint more often and display it everywhere in their castle.

It was a good thing their interaction hadn't been displayed

in the de Young. It would've been called *A Father's Shame,* and wouldn't have fit with the other, more whimsical pieces in the collection.

Clapping echoed from the main hall, followed by an announcement. Muffled voices struck her ears, though she couldn't make out any conversation in particular. As the speech ended, the crowd moved toward a glass case in the center of the floor. She couldn't tell what had been displayed.

"Why Bella Nolan?" Jack said from beside her.

The air froze in her lungs. "Excuse me?"

"Why are you determined to make *Werewolf in Venice* yours? Is it the painting in particular, or all Bella Nolan work?"

"Oh." For a second there, she thought Jack was asking about her nom de plume. As if he knew it was her. "I'm collecting her work for a private showing in Dublin."

Nodding, his lips pulled into a quick, contemplative frown. "Is that so?"

"You look confused."

He scrubbed his hands through his dark hair. "I'm not. But if you'd asked, I might've let you borrow the painting for the showing. You wouldn't have had to offer to buy it or come with me tonight—not that I don't appreciate your company. I donate paintings for showings all the time. Like tonight."

She'd thought about doing that at first, but the paintings were a gift for her father. A part of Isabelle secretly hoped her dad would fall in love with all of them and want them for himself. Besides, she wanted to take the work home, back to Dublin.

"I wanted it for personal reasons," she said, finishing her drink. "To appreciate it. No matter the cost."

. . .

Damn, the woman was stubborn. An unexpected surprise. He thoroughly enjoyed every snippy remark, every sly grin, every simmer of fire in her eyes.

It made him feel *alive.* Under the circumstances, he could use more of that.

As he thought of a rebuttal, the crowd clapped and mumbled again. This time, someone announced Jack's name over the microphone.

Why now? When he and Isabelle were finally getting somewhere?

"Would you give me one minute?" Taking the hand she'd dropped to her side, he squeezed gently. Starbursts of heat splintered into his palm. "I've got to do something. Don't disappear on me, okay? I'll be right back."

Something told him she wouldn't be going anywhere; she hadn't gotten the painting yet.

Dropping her hand, he moved through the crowd of smiling faces—recognizing not a single person—and his hands began to shake.

Not now. *Please* not now.

He approached the glass case and then turned, searching for Isabelle in the crowd. She'd stayed back. Far enough away that she wouldn't see his hands tremble.

"I hope you're all having a fabulous time tonight," Jack said, raising his near-empty glass. The ice rattled around inside as a tremor clattered through his arm. "I'd like to personally thank the de Young for their interest in this Renoir." *Hold strong. Don't show weakness.* "It's been a part of my collection for more years than I care to admit, and this is the first time it has seen the light of day. Or the glare of the moon, as it were." His vision swam in and out, in and out. Gripping the corner of the glass case for support, he rubbed his eyes. And stomach pains from hell rocked him. "Anyway, cheers."

Weaving through the crowd, Jack cursed and stumbled.

Fought his way back to Isabelle's side.

Another few minutes and he'd black out in front of everyone.

"Isabelle," he said, leaning against the nearest marble pillar. "I'm sorry to have to cut the night short, but something has come up. What hotel are you staying at tonight?"

"Are you okay? You look pale."

"I'm fine." *Focus on breathing. Air in, pause, air out.* "What's the name of your hotel?"

"The Grand Hyatt, but you look like you're going to—"

"Perfect," he rasped out, hollowing out in his middle. "I'll have the painting delivered to your hotel room in an hour. I'd like to make this up to you…if you'll let me, but it'll have to be at a later time."

And then, before he collapsed in the middle of the de Young, he staggered out the front doors and into the night.

Chapter Five

Isabelle drove her Camry back to the Grand Hyatt and hit every red light on the way. Her father used to say if she found herself stuck by a continuous string of red lights, it meant she subconsciously wanted to be going a different direction anyway. He said it was fate's way of giving chances to stop and rethink the route.

She wasn't sure she bought into it, but the constant stopping gave her a ton of time to think.

She still couldn't make sense of what happened between her and Jack.

They had chemistry; she'd felt it on her end, anyway.

He'd asked her to come to the museum, and then he up and left? What the hell was that about? She had to have missed something. His hands had started to tremble, she'd noticed that much. Was he nervous? Borderline drunk?

Regret washed over her in a bitter wave. Why'd it bother her so much that he took off and deserted her at his own artwork display, anyway? It wasn't like she wanted to spend the rest of the evening with him…

Trying not to think about Jack or what she wanted to do to him—*with him*, she corrected—she swapped her evening gown for yoga pants and washed her face. As she slipped into bed, someone banged on her bedroom door.

"Yes?" Shuffling over, she peeked through the peephole. "Who is it?"

A petite young woman with frizzy brown hair stood in the hall, holding up an awkward-shaped box.

"Hotel management," she said. "We have orders to drop something off to your room at precisely this hour. It's from Mr. Jack MacGrath?"

Jerking open the door, Isabelle met the manager with a smile. "Thank you," she said, and took the painting with more eagerness than was probably necessary. With another nod of thanks, she shut the door and swept inside to study her painting.

It was perfect, and finally coming home with her, and… there was a note pinned to the back.

She yanked it off and read aloud, "Isabelle, I'm sorry I had to run out on you tonight. That's not how I envisioned our first date ending."

Oh, go on, Mr. MacGrath…*how'd you really want to finish it?*

"I wanted to tell you earlier, but I have another piece of Bella Nolan art, *Werewolf in Manhattan.*"

Shut the front door.

"If you agree to have coffee with me tomorrow morning, the painting is yours. Please accept my sincere apology and meet me in front of your hotel at ten a.m. Jack."

Seriously? These two paintings were proving to be the easiest, cheapest finds ever. She would've paid millions to bring two of them home. But it seemed all she had to do was go on date number two with Jack.

Not such a bad deal considering he was the hottest man

she'd ever laid eyes on. Staring at him for another day didn't sound so bad.

She set up the painting on the desk across from the bed and let her eyes skip over its colors as she dozed off.

Except she woke up thirty minutes later and couldn't go back to sleep. She tossed and turned all night, thinking about how she was going to get all the paintings back. If only the other ten were as easy to snag as this one. She worried about how she'd display them in the National Gallery of Ireland, and what her father would say. When she crawled out of bed at nine, showered, and then dressed in jeans, black riding boots, a gray tank top, and a black cardigan, she still didn't have the answers to any of those things.

But she knew how to find one more painting, and it was waiting for her downstairs. In Jack's arms.

As she made her way into the lobby and then out the front doors, she searched one way and then the other. No sign of Jack. Sighing, she cinched her purse over her shoulder and waited.

"Isabelle," a deep voice called. "Over here."

Looking past the line of taxis, Isabelle spotted Jack standing in front of a black stretch limousine. He wore dark jeans, a deep blue sweater, and black boots. A shadow of stubble emphasized the rugged lines of his jaw and cheekbones. And there was a light in his eyes that hadn't been there yesterday. He appeared almost…hopeful, if she had to put her finger on it.

And in his hands were two Starbucks cups.

Delicious.

The coffee looked good, too.

• • •

"The note said you wanted to have coffee with me," she said, gazing out the passenger window of his limo. "Didn't we just take the exit for the San Francisco International Airport?"

As she turned to him, her hair fell over her shoulder in silky-soft waves. It took every ounce of willpower surging through Jack's veins not to reach out and brush a few loose strands out of her face.

Don't move too fast. You'll spook her.

"You're observant," he said, taking a long drink of his Americano. "We're taking a short flight to Napa."

"A—what?" She turned her full attention to him and glared. "Where are you taking me?"

"Napa. It's wine country, and we'll be back by tonight. You can leave after that if you want."

She quirked an eyebrow, though he didn't pick up one iota of resistance. "You didn't say anything about a flight."

"That's right, I didn't." The limo pulled into a private gate and swept around a large hangar. "But if you want the painting, that's where we have to go. I told you, it's not far. You'll be perfectly safe, if that's what you're worried about. We're going to visit a longtime friend of mine."

"Oh." She pinched her lips together with her forefinger and thumb. Contemplating. "And he has my painting?"

"*She*, actually. Her name is Jasmine Winters."

Isabelle stared out the window as if she were completely relaxed with the situation, yet his heightened sense of smell detected the rosy scent of curiosity, followed by subtle hints of jealousy.

It seemed Isabelle was piqued by his relationship with Jasmine.

"She's a sweetheart," he went on, trying to play it cool. "You'll love her."

"Oh, I'm sure I will." She cleared her throat, and adjusted her top. "So did you sell the painting to her, or…"

"About thirty years ago, she moved from New York to

San Francisco. She missed New York terribly, so I thought the painting would cheer her up." The limo stopped in front of his private jet. "I called her last night, asked if we could come up to grab it, and she said that was fine."

"Yes, fine," she said, though she didn't sound too enthusiastic about it.

He exited the limo, extending his hand to help her out. She took it, sending fiery spirals of heat snaking through his body. The surge of energy in his veins wasn't as strong as, say, a fight or a new adventure, but it was there. Satiating him. Giving him more time.

He'd been weakening more quickly the last few weeks—not that he'd admit it to a soul—and he didn't want to have to leave her again. Last night, he'd stumbled into the streets. Damn near been flattened by a Muni city bus. It still hadn't erased the queasy feeling in his gut, but it gave him enough strength to get home. After that, he rode his Ducati through the city streets. It'd been the fastest ride of his life. He'd almost died more times than he cared to count.

The only thing on his mind was having more time with Isabelle.

She couldn't go back to Ireland. Not yet.

"This is the plane we're taking?" She strode over the red carpet that'd been laid out. "What's with the grand entrance?"

"Branson got overexcited." Reluctantly releasing her hand, Jack finished off his coffee. "It's not often I have a woman come aboard."

"Oh, really?" Her gaze shot to his. "How often is often? No wait, forget I said anything."

Rather than answer, he spread his arms wide and guided her toward the small aircraft. "After you."

She ducked inside—giving him an unobstructed view of her curves—and took the seat nearest the window. He sat beside her and leaned back in his swivel chair.

"Never," he said finally.

"I'm sorry?"

"Never." He buckled in as the door shut behind them and the engines warmed. "I've never taken a woman anywhere in my jet."

"Oh," she said, meeting his stare. Pleasure flared in the depths of her eyes. "But if you did, I bet the red carpet treatment would make women fall head over heels in love with you."

"I'm not concerned about getting women to fall in love with me."

"Is that so?" She quirked an eyebrow. "Because if I recall, you were quick to cry fated wolf the first time we met."

"That was different…that was with you," he said simply, catching her gentle intake of breath at the words. "While we're on the topic, do you have a love interest back home?"

Say no, say no.

Even though there was only one Luminary—one fated mate—for each werewolf in existence, it didn't mean he or she was going to be celibate until the mate arrived. Quite the contrary, or so he'd heard in certain circles. There were werewolves who liked to have sex with as many partners as possible *before* meeting their Luminary. That way, when they finally met the person they were going to be with for the next thousand years, they would've already played the field.

He'd never had that urge.

He'd been too busy building an empire. Collecting valuable property and art. Traveling the world. Seeing new sights and broadening his horizons. He wasn't a saint—not by a long shot—but he never saw the advantage of whoring around while waiting for his mate.

Merely thinking about Isabelle having lovers in Ireland had the threat of a growl rumbling in the back of his throat.

"I don't have time for a boyfriend."

The tightening that'd been in his chest moments before loosened. She caught his eye as if she'd picked up the sudden comfort in him. She took her time finishing off her coffee as they taxied down the runway.

"And if I do find time," she continued, "my father finds a thousand reasons why I shouldn't be involved with someone who isn't my fated mate."

But I'm right here…

"My father is pretty strict on what I can and can't do." Clutching the armrests of her chair, she laid her head back as they lifted off. With a bump and a groan of the engines, they were soaring through the air. "I'm sorry, I'm not particularly fond of planes, and I talk when I'm nervous. Stop me if I'm blabbering too much."

"That would never happen." He hadn't meant to say it aloud, but there it was. "I like listening to your voice. It's soothing."

Sliding her head over the headrest, she glanced at him. "So is yours."

A moment passed between them, charged with smoldering heat. The air crackled, causing his heart to jump. And then just like that, she severed eye contact, and the moment was gone.

"I'm going to be Alpha of the Irish Wolf Pack after my father. Did I tell you that?"

He shook his head, desperately trying to recapture that moment. Every now and again, when she wasn't nervous or trying to peg him for a scoundrel, she opened up. Only then could he glimpse the real Isabelle Connelly hidden behind the walls she'd put up. She had a great sense of humor, and a stubborn flair that kept him on his toes.

If she was his forever, it was going to be a hell of a lot of fun.

As she continued to talk about her father, her voice cracked. She would rule the pack and follow in his shoes, no doubt. She'd probably run it with the same values, too. When they first met, she'd been so eager to think the worst of him—and how could he blame her? His family had treated their werewolf brothers and sisters as pawns to expand their own businesses in the States. He'd tried to shed their reputation by building one of his own, but it seemed her father hadn't forgotten…and had made sure his heir apparent wouldn't, either.

Everything made sense: her hesitation, the distance she kept, the walls she continually tried to put up, and the bitterness that trickled into her tone every now and again.

Reality was a nasty son of a bitch.

"I spend most of my day studying Irish tradition and wolf pack law. He wants me well-versed in the history of the pack, from its origination in the 1500s up to modern practices."

On the short flight to Napa County Airport, they talked about her pack and the family dynamic they'd instilled. Everyone genuinely cared about one another. It was refreshing, since he'd had only Branson to depend on for the last hundred years. Fraternizing with other werewolves from the San Francisco Wolf Pack simply didn't sound appealing.

Hayden Dean, the Alpha of his pack, always sent him a personal invite to all of the wolf pack events, but he'd hardly accepted.

Especially not in the last twenty years.

Everyone could sense he was an unmated wolf. Past the three-hundred-year mark, he'd sensed their pity, their willingness to help, and their inability to do so.

That had been the breaking point.

No one was going to feel sorry for him.

"And then, after a while, I reached the point where he told me about the restrictions with my Luminary," she said plainly.

The plane started its descent as his stomach whirled.

"What restrictions?"

"Since I'm the Alpha's only heir and my Luminary will rule the pack with me, he's got to be someone from the Irish Wolf Pack."

Sucker punch to the gut.

"That's a bit shortsighted, don't you think?"

"How so?" The plane's wheels touched down with a loud *screech*. "If my mate is from another pack, he wouldn't know a thing about the traditional way we run things. He could learn, but it wouldn't be in him. He wouldn't have the trust of the pack."

"But you can't chose who you're fated to love."

"You're right." She worried her bottom lip between her teeth as they taxied to a stop near the small terminal. "But you can choose to live alone rather than bond with someone who doesn't have the pack's best interest at heart."

Wow. "That's harsh, don't you think?"

"Harsh?"

"You'd live three hundred years"—give or take twenty, depending on the amount of adrenaline in her system—"and die young rather than bond with someone you're destined to be with? What's worse is you'll be condemning me to an early death, too."

It was ridiculous. Inexcusable.

She shook her head slowly as the plane door opened and cool air whipped through the cabin. "I'm not condemning *you* to death. I don't know why you're worried about something that hasn't even happened and doesn't concern you."

"Because you're wrong. It does concern me." His heartbeat pounded in his ears. "It may not have hit you full force yet, the way it has for me, but it's there. Deep down, on some level, you know it."

She didn't move. Not a muscle. Not a quiver or a twitch of those perfect lips.

She *did* feel it.

"Mr. MacGrath?" the steward blurted from the rear of the plane. "The Porsche you requested has arrived."

"Porsche?" That got Isabelle twirling around in her chair and peering out the tiny oval window. "*That*…is what we're driving to your friend's house?"

"It's a Porsche 911 GT2 RS."

"Yeah." She chuckled. "Whatever that means."

The car was black as night. Fin on the back. Six hundred and twenty horsepower. Sleek and mean, with the smooth, gliding curves of a sexy woman.

"It's the fastest street-legal model on the market." Jack shrugged, itching to push it to its limit. "If we have to take a drive through wine country, might as well do it in style, right?" He smirked as the steward extended the keys toward him. "Care to see how fast it can go?"

"Hell yes." Standing with lightning-quick speed, Isabelle snatched the keys out of the steward's hand. "And I'm driving."

Chapter Six

Jack could barely focus on his GPS. "Turn right."

Isabelle shifted, barreling around a sharp curve.

"Hard left."

Pedal to the metal, she did as she was told and gripped the wheel tight. The car hugged the bend effortlessly, even though they buried the speed limit.

"Up ahead," he said over the powerful purr of the engine. "One mile. Winery is on the right."

But the winery came faster than she anticipated.

Guess that's what happened when you drove one hundred–plus.

"Right here." Jack's voice constricted. "You're going to miss it."

"No, I'm not." She downshifted, causing the engine to roar. "Hold on."

Braking hard, she waited until the car was below sixty, and then released the brake and turned right. The car lost traction, and exhilaration filled her right up. Jack gripped her knee, squeezing tight. Glancing at him out of the corner of her eye, she recovered from the skid, shifted again, and came to a sudden stop in front of a Tuscan-style home. Tall pillars. Stone moldings on the front. Soft mood lighting, even in the daylight. And now that she had the chance to check out her surroundings, grapevines stretched out as far as the eye could see.

Leaning over, Jack yanked the keys out of the ignition. "I think I'll take these."

She giggled, but as his hand brushed her knee she went hot. "Did I scare you?" she asked, rubbing the spot that was still tingling from his touch.

"It was just what I needed."

What'd he mean by that?

Before she could pry, he opened the door and got out, stretching. She followed, meeting him on the passenger side of the car. Out of morbid curiosity, she checked his hands. They had been shaking last night, after all. Now, they were still and sure.

Strange.

"Jack!" a woman's voice called from the direction of the front door. Her accent was thick. Spanish, maybe? Italian mixed with a little Greek? "Get over here and give me a hug."

"Great to see you, Jasmine."

He waltzed over and scooped her up into a huge embrace. As he spun her around, Isabelle got a good look at Jack's "friend." His *only* friend, it seemed. Branson excluded, of course. Jasmine was taller than her. Probably five foot nine. Razor-short blond hair, falling around her face and framing her chin. And she was skinny with boobs, damn it. Wearing a flowery maxi dress, a cropped jean jacket, and wedge sandals.

Some things in life weren't fair.

"The place looks amazing," Jack said. "As do you."

When he set her down, she nudged him with her elbow and then pointed at Isabelle. "Going to introduce me to your lady?"

Your lady?

She wasn't his any more than the Porsche cooling off behind them.

A hint of sadness pricked her, making her frown. Shaking it off, Isabelle stepped up onto Jasmine's patio and extended her hand. "I'm Isabelle Connelly. We're looking for a Bella Nolan painting, *Werewolf in Manhattan*."

Jack rolled his eyes. "She's bound and determined to find pieces to add to her collection in Dublin. It's all she talks about."

"Oh, I see." Jasmine shot Jack a perfect smile. "But why don't you just—"

"Do you have it inside?" Jack cut her off, touching her arm as he spoke. "Would you mind if we saw it first thing?"

Isabelle's gaze homed in on his touch. He held Jasmine's arm, just above the elbow. His touch was gentle and reassuring, his fingers lightly brushing against her skin. A low hum rumbled through Isabelle's belly.

It was the strangest thing: coffee didn't normally give her indigestion.

"If you're ready," Jasmine said, starting into the house. "It's right this way."

Eager to set eyes on her painting, Isabelle strode inside before Jack and was instantly taken aback. The entire place was covered in white marble sculptures. Small pieces stood on windowsills. Larger ones were situated in the foyer, and in the corners of the great hall that led to the living area. More sculptures greeted them there. There were angels, kings, and couples lost in loving embraces.

"Your home is stunning." She couldn't help but traipse slowly, taking in every inch. "How long did it take you to collect all these?"

"Better part of two hundred years. Jack helped me find this

one." She brushed her hand along a sculpture of Aphrodite as she passed. "Remember the auctioneer winking at you?"

He chuckled. "I remember."

"You could've had any woman you wanted," Jasmine said, shooting Jack a sideways glance.

Isabelle could've mistaken the gleam in her eye, but Jasmine sounded…jaded.

"But you pushed everyone away," she continued with a sigh, and then turned her attention to Isabelle as they wound through the formal dining room. "He's a loner, this one. Better guard your heart."

"Oh, don't worry," he blurted from beside her. "She's built up Fort Knox around it. No one's getting in."

Jasmine chuckled. "You sound as if you've tried."

Isabelle glanced at Jack out of the corner of her eye. His jaw clenched and unclenched. His lips pressed white. And then he met her gaze. Though his body was tense and his movements jerky, there was a softness in his eyes that contradicted all of it.

As they strode down a narrow hall that smelled of rose petals and vanilla, Jasmine said, "I keep the painting in the bedroom. It reminds me of the city I love so much."

Did they have a tryst in New York? Isabelle couldn't help but wonder. Pangs assaulted her stomach again as the thought struck her.

Jasmine opened the door and they swept inside into a world of white. White bedding, pillows, fluffy blankets. White floors, furniture, and curtains.

And there, on the wall over the Ice Queen's bed, hung *Werewolf in Manhattan*. The only splash of color in the pristinely monochromatic room. She couldn't help but hold her breath.

It was as beautiful as she remembered. The city had been buzzing with excitement that night, so she and Neil had gone to a rooftop so they had a breathtaking view of the unmistakable skyline and no one to interrupt them.

Isabelle hadn't realized it, but she'd walked over to the bed to get a better view. When she realized she'd been staring for too long, she twirled around. Jack and Jasmine stood near the door, whispering.

. . .

"Something I missed?" Isabelle asked sweetly.

Oh, she could play it cool now, but jealousy burned in her gorgeous green eyes.

She may not have wanted to admit it, and hell if he knew how he was doing it, but he was getting through to her. Finally getting under her skin. If only there was a way to speed up the process. Make her realize how great they could be together, especially if that was the way fate had intended.

"Jack was just telling me that you're from Ireland," Jasmine said, climbing over the bed to take the painting off the wall. "That you're going to be the Alpha of the pack."

"That's right."

Jasmine unhooked the art and handed it to Jack.

"Sounds wonderful. I've always wanted to visit Ireland." As Jasmine slid off the bed, she put an arm around Isabelle's shoulder. "What do you say we talk about it over lunch?"

"I don't know," Jack said, checking his watch. "Now that we have the painting, we should probably get back."

"Nonsense." Isabelle followed Jasmine toward the kitchen. "I wouldn't mind talking about Ireland, as long as you tell me a little about how you know Jack."

Shit.

"No, we really should—"

"Oh, I'll give you *all* his juicy secrets." Jasmine beamed, glancing over her shoulder at him as they walked past. "I'll make cream cheese chicken and grilled asparagus. Does that sound all right?"

No, none of that sounded remotely close to "all right." Okay, the cream cheese chicken sounded bomb.

Despite the resistance flaring in him, he followed the women anyway, confused as hell how they went from strangers to best friends in two seconds flat.

Jasmine was all business in the kitchen, sweeping from the countertop grill to the sink, and back to the island where he and Isabelle were seated. She put the asparagus on the grill, drizzled it with oil and spices, and then went to work seasoning the chicken. For a few minutes, Jack thought he was in the clear.

"Jack and I met at a sorority house," she announced, stirring spices.

Here we go.

Resting his elbows on the granite, he tented his fingers together and listened. Isabelle did the same, as if she were mocking him. And when he glanced at her out of the corner of his eye, she bumped him. The playful move lit him up inside, sparking a smile and a feeling of lightness that hadn't been there before.

"That was a few years after I moved back to San Francisco. About"—she patted the chicken and stared off into space—"twenty-eight years ago, I guess. Let me tell you, Jack MacGrath was on the prowl."

He grimaced. "Do we really have to go into this?"

"Yes," the women blurted in unison. And then they smiled.

"He wouldn't take anyone home, though. Oh no. He would go to the parties at the werewolf sorority houses on SFSU's campus, have a drink, introduce himself, stay for a few hours, and then bolt. Never stayed with one woman long enough to have anything serious, even if he hadn't found his mate." She threw the chicken on a second grill next to the first. This one had high sides. "Can you believe it?"

Isabelle shook her head and bumped him again. "Sorority houses? Is that where you were looking for your Luminary?"

"One place among many." His voice sounded solemn, though he hadn't meant it to. "I searched for years."

He held her gaze longer than necessary to drive the point home. He didn't want just anyone. He wanted her. And now that he had found her, he wasn't letting her go.

"He wasn't very charming back then, if you can believe it." Jasmine wagged a spatula at him before turning the chicken. "But along the way, everything flipped on its end."

"He wasn't very charming *back then*?" Isabelle parroted, grinning. "As if something changed?"

The hair on the back of his neck stood on end. "I'd rather not talk about it."

Jasmine stood with her back to them, hand on her hip, staring at the chicken. And then, after a few moments, she dumped cream cheese, heavy cream, and milk into the pan.

It was a heart attack in the making, but smelled tasty.

"He used to go out more, but would have this apathetic, almost grumpy expression on his face. For years. Remember, Jack?" Pouting into a frown, she raised her shoulders up and looked as if she were giving her best imitation of Grumpy Cat. "Like this."

Isabelle cracked up beside him. "That's a good impression."

"Jasmine…"

"But then he bought two Bella Nolan paintings." Taking the asparagus off the grill, she rolled a few onto each plate and then flipped the coated chicken onto the top. "He stopped going out, but when I'd stop by to check on him, he seemed happy. As if the paintings truly eased whatever pain he was hiding inside."

"Oh, that's deep, Jasmine," he said, staring at his food the second she slid it over the island. "Is that what your psychology degree did for you?"

She shrugged, standing across from them with her own plate. "Am I off base?"

Isabelle's gaze flipped between them.

"It's reaching," he answered quickly.

"Umm-hmm," Jasmine mumbled, her cheeks full of chicken. "That's why you gave me *Werewolf in Manhattan*, wasn't it?"

"Why?" Isabelle said, scooting closer—so close their arms brushed, sending chills through him. "Why'd you give it to her?"

"So I wouldn't feel so lonely," Jasmine answered for him. "If it worked for him, so he didn't feel lonely without his Luminary, it would work for me."

As he chewed slowly, trying to keep food in his mouth so he didn't have to talk, Isabelle's gaze heated the side of his face.

"Which was why I was so surprised when he called, saying he was going to give the paintings to you. It's not that I mind giving it up—it was never mine to begin with—but he'd held on so tightly for so long"—she set down her fork and bent over the island—"and then he shows up with you, and I understand."

Isabelle's heart slowed—he could hear its strumming beat, calling him.

"You understand what?" Isabelle said softly.

Jasmine's eyes sparked with dark amusement. "She really doesn't know, does she?"

He shook his head and choked down the last bite of food. It was tastier than it smelled, creamy and flavorful. He swallowed down a helping of despair, too, while he was at it.

"Forget it," Jasmine said with a smile while turning on her

charm. "Enough about Jack and me, and Bella Nolan. Which part of Ireland are you from?"

They talked for hours about Ireland and San Francisco and New York and places they'd never been that they'd always wanted to go. He hadn't realized it was nearly four o'clock, but the tremors rattling through his fingers served as a personal alarm clock.

They were coming closer now.

"Time to go," he said, and hustled her out the front door.

With *Werewolf in Manhattan* in one hand, Isabelle embraced Jasmine in a bear hug with the other and kissed her on the cheek. They certainly took their sweet time to say good-bye.

Not like they had a ticking timer counting down the last minutes of their life, or anything...

"She's the one," Jasmine whispered into Jack's ear when they embraced. "I think she might be the only one who can't see it."

He nodded in total agreement and turned to stride toward the car. His stomach seized into a knot. His vision swam and his hands went numb.

Not now.

"You drive," he said, digging into his pocket and throwing Isabelle the keys.

Wouldn't want to have a seizure on the road and put them both in jeopardy.

Her face lit up as she stowed the painting in the trunk. "You sure you want me to drive again?"

If he got the feeling he was going to die again, hell yes.

It'd give him just the rush he needed to make it back to the city.

She drove the Porsche hard and fast, exactly the way he'd needed her to. She'd tried to make small talk, but he had to stay focused on slowing his heart rate. Surges of energy pulsed through him, smoothing out the shakes. But the nausea remained. And his vision was still off. There were two Isabelles in his sights—not that having two of her wouldn't be amazing in certain scenarios.

"Are you okay, Jack?" she asked as they pulled up to the airport. "Every now and again your color looks off. You look...gray."

His vision cleared, only for a moment. "I'm fine."

Or at least he would be.

The flight back to San Francisco was a blur. Had he dozed off? Stared into space? Gawked at Isabelle's legs the whole time? He couldn't say.

And it spooked the hell out of him.

Shakes, seizures, and blackouts. That was the order of things the medicine man had discussed. He'd yet to have a blackout, but couldn't explain what had just happened.

He had to do something before it was too late.

As the plane taxied to where Branson was waiting with the limo, Jack leaned over and tapped Isabelle on the shoulder. She turned to him with more attitude than he'd expected.

She'd probably tried to talk to him during the flight, and he'd probably tuned out.

Perfect.

"I'm sorry about the way things ended tonight," he said, though he fumbled the last words. Jumbled them together a bit. "I'm going to take a cab home, and have Branson take you back to your hotel. I don't know how long you plan to stay, but there's something else I'd like to show you. Would you wait? Another day, at least?"

He needed a stiff burn of adrenaline rocketing through his veins, like now. Maybe after he did that, he'd surprise Isabelle at her hotel. He'd have Branson get her number before dropping her off.

Her mouth downturned. "Why would we part ways here?

At the airport? And why wouldn't Branson just take you home?"

Too many questions.

And he simply didn't want her to see him this way, at his worst and weakest.

Damn it, why'd he have to be borderline blackout now?

"I'm sorry," he said, and kissed her hand before rushing down the back stairs.

Chapter Seven

Isabelle had everything she needed. *Werewolf in Venice.* *Werewolf in Manhattan.* A limousine ride at her disposal, on Jack's dime.

But for some reason, she couldn't make up her mind where to go.

Okay, okay, so her mind was totally made up. It was a tiny tug in the pit of her stomach that kept her stuck in IndecisionLand.

"Where to, miss?" Branson asked for the second time. Glancing at her through the rearview mirror, Jack's butler raised his bushy eyebrows in expectation. "Where would you like me to drop you off?"

"Does he do this often?"

He frowned. "I'm sorry? I'm not sure I understand."

Adjusting the painting beside her on the leather seat, Isabelle stared out the window at his private jet in the distance. Jack had already taken off, darting into one of the terminals to "take a cab home."

Ridiculous.

As if she'd believe that line of crap.

He was probably waiting for her to leave so he could fly back to Jasmine's.

"Does he take women on day trips with his jet, and then run off unexpectedly before the night's over?"

Branson stared, giving nothing away with those flat gray eyes. The guy was handsome, but looked like a dolt when he just *sat* there.

She slid forward on the seat. "How many women have you given rides home this way?"

"Just you, miss." Branson started the engine. "Where to?"

Isabelle slouched into the seat with a huff.

She was the only woman he'd left this way?

Well, that stung.

"Is he flying anywhere else tonight?" she asked. *To Jasmine's,* she meant.

"No, miss. They're taking the jet back to the hangar now." He pointed out the window. "Take a look."

He was right. So what the hell? What had she done wrong?

"Jack isn't going home, is he?" she asked, tapping her fingers against her mouth.

A long, drawn-out pause, and then, "No, miss."

"I knew it. Where'd he go?" She slid to the edge of her seat. "Please, Branson. Tell me where I can find him."

"He enjoys a good boxing match every now and again." Finally, Branson glanced over his shoulder. And winked. "I believe there's an open ring on Judah Street that he likes to frequent."

"Thanks, Branson," she said, and held on for the ride.

A good forty minutes later, they turned on Judah Street. When he stopped in front of a gym that looked perfectly normal—and closed—she exhaled heavily.

"It's closed. See the sign?" She pointed. "He must be

somewhere else. Any other ideas?"

"Not everything is as it seems, miss." He parked on the street in front and put the car in park. "I'll wait for you here."

Hesitant, Isabelle slid out, leaving the painting behind in his safekeeping. In parts of downtown Dublin, she might've been frightened walking around by herself in the evening. But San Francisco was alive at night. Illuminated with possibility. Cars honked and sped through red lights, and the bars were still overflowing.

Isabelle peeked in the windows of Kicking Kango's. It was dark inside, and not a single scent of a werewolf tingled her nose.

"Where are you?" she whispered, turning back to the street. "This can't be it, but Branson said..."

And then she heard it.

A guttural moan. Scratches of claws through flesh. Muffled cheering.

Couldn't be right...

Moving along the side of the Kicking Whatever, Isabelle tiptoed, listening. More of the same. Hissing and spitting. A low roar. Clapping? The sounds were primal, raw and real. And they were coming from the basement. From out of nowhere, the scent of a wolf struck her.

The tallest, largest guy—scratch that...*werewolf*—that she'd ever seen turned the corner. She startled, hugging the wall of the building. It wasn't his size that had her holding her breath as he passed by, though he was well over six feet six, three hundred pounds of pure muscle. No, it was the blood trickling down his temples that had her staring bug-eyed.

"Evening." He spoke as if he were going on a nice nightly stroll. As if the blood trickling down his temples hadn't just dripped onto his collared shirt.

She swallowed hard. "Good evening."

Keeping her eye on him, Isabelle weaved around the

corner and faced a heavy door. The guy had to have come from here. Unless he was Dumpster diving. But there wasn't any garbage back here for him to dig in.

A sharp cry split the night, followed by the unmistakable stench of testosterone. It burned her nose, dark and crisp. And then a wave of Jack's scent hit her. It was musky and crisp, and made her stomach tighten.

Without thinking, she knocked on the door. It opened a sliver, and a man's face—beady black eyes, wide nose, thin lips—filled the space. He was a werewolf, young and stupid, from the reckless smell of him.

"Yes?" He looked her up and down and sniffed the air, checking to make sure she was one of his kind. "Admission for one is fifty. Cash only."

"Admission?" She shook cobwebs out of her head. "For what?"

Growling floated through the sliver in the door, followed by a pained moan.

The man's beady eyes shifted into the room behind him and then back to her. "Someone must've told you about our underground werewolf fight club. You're here, aren't ya?"

"Werewolf"—she lowered her voice as the word punched out of her—"fight club?" How twisted. Is this what the werewolves in the city did when they were bored? What Neanderthals they were. Members of the Irish Wolf Pack would never participate in anything this barbaric. "No, I don't want to come in. I was looking for Jack MacGrath. Do you know if he's in there somewhere?"

"Oh, he's here all right." He barked out a sinister laugh. "But he's in no shape to come out and talk to ya."

What did that mean? Was he drunk? Passed out?

"Do you mind if I come in to talk to him myself? I'll only be a minute."

"If you pay the cost of admission, you can talk to him all

damned night."

Rolling her eyes, Isabelle fished sixty dollars out of her purse. The doorman pocketed the bills. And kept her change. She felt his eyes on her back as she entered, and then descended down a set of narrow stairs. Clearly, if there was a fight club happening downstairs after hours, the business was San Francisco Wolf Pack owned and maintained.

Couldn't they do anything better with their time and money?

Her ears detected the sounds of clashing bodies and teeth tearing into flesh. The floor vibrated beneath her feet as sounds of fighting rumbled off the walls.

Heart in her throat, she reached the bottom of the stairs. The entire basement opened up into a giant padded room. Fluorescent lights flickered overhead. Beams split the open space. Other than that, there wasn't a single piece of furniture. Or maybe it was the grouping of large, shouting men blocking her view.

There were too many bodies to count, huddled against one another, hollering toward the center of the room. The gagging mixture of sweat, bloody fur, testosterone, and pure anger created a fog that lingered on the air, choking her.

"Disgusting," she muttered, putting a hand to her nose to block the direct flow of the stench. "So gross."

A few men turned around, glaring, as if she'd been talking about them. They weren't the type to mess with. Bald heads and bare chests. Covered in dark tats and scars.

"Oh, I'm sorry, I didn't mean you two." She flushed hot. "Of course not. You're not disgusting. I meant your smell. Well, not *your* smell, but the collective smell."

Shut up, shut up.

They glowered, their eyes narrowing to slits.

"I'm just going to"—she moved away, putting up her hands—"go find a spot to stand over here and look for my friend. My very large, mean biker friend."

Strangled with fear, it was the only thing she could think to say, but the second she was free from their heated gazes, she laughed. One of her nervous, scared laughs, but still.

And no sign of Jack.

The crowd booed, pumping their fists in the air over their heads.

Standing on tiptoe, she tried to get a glimpse at the center of the room, but no way. Not from this angle against these burly men. And she couldn't fit between them.

As she moved through the raging mob, Isabelle realized every man in the place was bare-chested. Most were covered in scars and sweat. And every single one of them was so preoccupied by what was happening in the center of the room that they barely recognized her presence.

When she reached the back wall, a place she felt safe so no one could steal behind her, she bumped against a wood crate. *Perfect.* Stepping up, she looked out into the room, eager to get a vantage point to better look for Jack.

The quicker the better, so she could get the hell out of here.

Two wolves tangled in the center of the room.

She gasped, watching in horror as they reared up on their back haunches and crashed into each other with brutal force. They growled, baring their teeth as they clashed them together.

The guy at the door had said this was a werewolf fight club, but with the men surrounding the room, she hadn't actually expected the men to be fighting as *wolves.*

Right in the middle of the city.

Covering her mouth with her hand, Isabelle gawked, unable to detach her gaze from the horror of the fight.

One of the wolves—the sleeker one with the raven-black hair—was covered in a mess of sweat and blood. His fur was matted down the back, wet and dark red. His face was bashed in on the right side , and the tip of his nose had been sliced open by a claw.

The other wolf—the auburn-haired, much larger one—had claw marks streaking down his left side and was bleeding over one of his eyes. Other than that, he was fine.

Colliding with cruelly intense force, the wolves bit and clawed. Jumped back. When one leaped, the other matched. Blood gushed over the floor as the auburn wolf sliced through the side of the darker.

He howled in agony.

The men in the crowd bellowed, a roll of thunder that vibrated the entire building. Isabelle's heart drummed in her chest.

Limping and bleeding, the darker wolf attacked. As their massive bodies slammed together, the darker wolf slipped in a pool of his own blood. Taking advantage, the auburn wolf leaped on top of the other and pinned him to the ground.

Although the auburn wolf clearly had the upper hand in strength and size—and now, position—the darker wolf was the one who wouldn't quit attacking. He snapped with sheer anger. He was focused. Determined to fight to the end, it seemed, no matter the cost to him.

Well, she figured, they could simply shift when the injuries became too much to bear. Maybe that's how the fight ended. When one wolf couldn't take the pain anymore and shifted back, it must've been the equivalent of screaming mercy.

They'd heal.

Everyone would head home.

It was still barbaric, but at least no one would have any lasting injuries. As she scanned the room, her gaze settled on the backs of a few men crowding near the fight. They were terribly scarred.

These fighters would live, but be marred forever? For the

fun of it?

Yeah, forget barbaric. They were just stupid. Testosterone-raging idiots.

Speaking of, where was Jack in all this?

A guttural cry jerked her attention back to the fight. The darker wolf was still pinned, its feet pushing against the larger wolf's chest. It didn't look good.

Severing the carotid artery could kill a werewolf. A bite to the neck from another wolf would do it. And from the way the auburn wolf's teeth were poised at the neck of the darker wolf, he was threatening to do real damage.

"Come on, MacGrath," someone yelled from the front. "I've got three grand riding on your ass."

MacGrath?

Jack.

But where? In the fight? No…

Desperation streaking through her, Isabelle scanned the horde of half-naked men. From this angle, they all looked the same. Thick, muscular bodies slickened with sweat.

She'd never find him.

"Get off the ground," the same person roared. "Put up a fight!"

Her stomach dropped.

She'd come here to figure out why he kept ditching her at the end of all their dates. But clearly he had bigger issues…

"Jack?"

Her voice carried too easily through the room. It must've been the high pitch against the grumbling of the men. The swarm in front of her turned to glare. And as they moved, they created an alley for Isabelle to get a clear shot of the darker wolf—*Jack*—on the ground.

She squealed as the auburn wolf reared up, teeth bared. Ready to sink its teeth into his neck.

"Jack, get up!"

As if her voice made a direct shot from her lips to his ears, he twitched. Writhed beneath the auburn wolf. And craned around to search for her in the crowd. In that split second of distraction, the auburn wolf sliced his paw across Jack's neck. He howled, a sinister sound that hurt her ears.

The mob went silent as blood squirted from his neck.

Shift back, shift back, shift back.

Slowly, the auburn wolf released him and backed off. Jack didn't move. As the crowd dispersed, Isabelle fought her way to the front. Disgust wormed its way through her. Watch the fight, scream and make bets, and when someone falls to the ground dead, walk away.

They weren't barbarians. They were cowards.

"Jack," she said, kneeling at his side. "Can you hear me?"

He was covered in gunk—blood, sweat, and drool, probably—so she didn't want to touch him. Ghosting her hand over his neck, she could've sworn her heart hiccuped in her chest.

He'd heal if he shifted back. But if he was knocked out cold…he could die lying here in a pool of his own blood.

"Someone help him," she called out. But everyone was filing out. Not a care in the world if one of their packmates suffered a lethal blow. "Please, someone help!"

He was losing too much blood.

Heart thumping out of her chest, Isabelle did the only thing she could think to do. She covered his wound with her hand. Put as much pressure as she could to stop the bleeding. His fur was soft—not coarse, as she would've imagined it to be—and wet, sliding between her fingers. He had large brown eyes, though they'd closed, and long lashes resting against his furry face. And he was larger up close. Not small, as she'd thought from her vantage point at the back of the room. He was muscular, but lean. Undeniably strong.

Although he was a jerk for leaving her—twice—and

really freaking stupid to put himself in this position, he was striking in wolf form. Not that she'd ever tell him that.

"You can't die, MacGrath," she said, adding more pressure to the wound. "I'm not finished bothering you yet."

At her words, Jack coughed and hacked up a bunch of blood on the concrete.

Thank God, he was alive.

With a sigh, she cradled his big head in her hands. "You're going to be all right." She swore. "Can you hear me? Just find the energy to shift back."

He opened his eyes and blinked up at her. There was a tenderness in his wide wolf eyes that tugged at her heart. A vulnerability that weaseled its way into her chest and squeezed.

"You're a git," she said, going warm and tingly all over. "I just want you to know that before I save your life."

And then his head went limp in her hands.

Chapter Eight

Jack clawed his way out of the darkness. Barely. It was Isabelle's scent that finally pulled him through. All through the night, she surrounded him. He tried to rouse enough to talk and ask her to stay, but couldn't muster the strength.

It wasn't until sunlight pierced his eyelids that he finally awoke.

Feeling like he'd been beaten with a baseball bat, Jack used all his strength to move his head around over the pillow. The curtains to his room were wide open, letting in the full glare of the morning sun. Isabelle had curled up in the chair beside his bed, her head dropped forward and her eyes closed. She'd changed into a bulky black sweater, black leggings, and hot-pink slippers that looked like mops.

Where the hell did she find slippers like that? Nineteen ninety-five?

A black duffel bag slouched against the side of her chair, and a sketchbook rested in her lap, flipped to a page with a pencil image on it. Reaching over, Jack slid the book off her lap and propped it up on his knees. He'd just started flipping when she snatched the sketchbook out of his hand and closed it.

"Aren't you a nosy one," she said with a yawn. "You must be feeling better."

"I didn't know you sketched."

"It's a hobby." Her eyes shifted to the sketchpad, and then back to him. "A way to keep my hands busy when I'm bored."

Sighing, he rested his head back against the pillows. "You're bored, yet you're still here."

"I am."

Chills scattered over his skin at her words.

"I couldn't leave until I knew you were going to come out of this." She ran her fingers through her hair, and then let the silky-soft layers fall around her face. Sunlight hit her from behind, creating a soft halo of gold around her head. "Despite what you may think, I'm not totally heartless."

Rising off the chair, she leaned over the bed and touched his forehead. He flinched at first, until he realized she was checking a bandage there. Her touch was gentle—the most soothing caress he'd ever felt in his life. It was as if the warmth in her hand bloomed through his entire body.

"I never thought you were heartless." He eyed her carefully as she tended to him. "A horrible driver? Yes. Absolutely."

Dabbing a cloth in a bowl beside the bed, Isabelle pulled back the sheet and touched it to his side. "I was driving fast, but in control. I'm *not* a bad driver."

"The fountain in my front yard begs to differ."

She squeaked in shock. "I was distracted by the—you know what? I'm not hashing this out again. I already told you I'll pay to replace your Monument of Manhood."

Hissing, he recoiled from the cold as it dampened his skin. It struck him that she was comfortable tending to him— had she done it all night? From the recesses of his mind, the memory of her touch skated forward.

She'd been here. All night. Caring for him when he was hurt.

For someone who claimed to loathe him, nursing his wounds was a strange move...

The duffel bag resting beside the chair must've been hers, he realized. Branson must've brought her things from the hotel so she'd be comfortable here. He'd have to thank Branson later for taking care of Isabelle.

"It's going to take a high-pressure hose to get all the dried blood off you," she said. "And you're going to have scars. Not on your face, but here." She touched his abs, sending pinpricks of delight scattering down to his groin. "And here."

And lower...

With a visible shiver, Isabelle replaced the cloth and folded her arms over her chest. "Care to explain the mental breakdown you had last night?"

"I don't recall a breakdown." But he remembered the adrenaline rush big-time. All it took was stepping into the ring with the largest werewolf in the place. One strike with the force of a hammer, one quick claw to his muzzle, and he'd gotten what he'd been looking for. How long the strength would last this time, he wasn't certain. "If you're talking about the fight, it was a way for me to blow off steam."

"No, it was more than that. It was suicide." She plopped into the seat once more and clutched the sketchbook against her. "I nearly had a canary watching you in there."

"A canary?" Chuckling, he shook his head. "That must've been painful. On account of the beak, and all."

"No, a canary, a fright—you know what? It's not about the way I talk." She narrowed her eyes at him. "After the fight, you passed out for over an hour. The bouncer had to call Branson to come get you. He and I dragged you to the car and brought you here. You could've died from your injuries."

She was right. "Why didn't I?"

"Branson gave you an epinephrine shot." Tired lines formed around her eyes. "You woke up startled for a few seconds, long enough to shift back. You collapsed and have been out since then."

"Shit."

He rubbed his thigh where he was still tender from the needle. He'd given up epinephrine shots years ago, after he'd gotten a skin infection that landed him in the hospital. And he couldn't get an adrenaline rush while lying in a hospital bed. So in order to avoid the impossible scenario, he'd avoided needles from that day on. He preferred more natural ways to get his high, anyway.

Getting shot with epinephrine wasn't always pretty. Neither was the fight. Yet she'd witnessed everything. More than that, she'd followed him to the gym, dragged him out when he was at his weakest, and remained by his bedside until he woke up.

How could he repay her?

"What *was* that?" she asked, penetrating him with those sultry green eyes. "Why would you leave before the end of our date, and hop into a fight with a werewolf ten times—"

"Wait, did you call it a date?"

Flustered, she batted her lids and shook her head. "What I was saying was you hopped into a fight with a werewolf ten times bigger than—"

"No, I heard what you said." A smile pulled at his lips. "You said before the end of our date."

She huffed and slouched into the chair. "Maybe I should've left you on the floor in that gym."

"I'm glad you didn't." Sitting upright against the headboard, he used his heightened sense of hearing to listen for her heartbeat. It was racing. Thumping loud in her rib cage. She might not have known it yet, but it called for him.

"Because if you'd left me there, I wouldn't have seen how radiant you are in the early-morning light."

She softened, her head lolling to her shoulder. "You can stop with the flirting. It wasn't a date. I misspoke. And you seem to think I'll forget about the question at hand."

"Which one is that?"

"Why'd you shift from this really great guy at Jasmine's to Muhammad Ali? You ran out like your clothes were on fire. At first I thought you might've been offended by something Jasmine said about your attachment to Bella Nolan's paintings, but now I don't think that's it." She stood and moved toward the windows. He had an excellent view of the city from there. "You acted like you didn't want to leave me at the airport, but then I can't imagine anyone wanting to get their head bashed in by a werewolf in an underground fight club, so you really didn't want to do either of those things. Yet here you are, two inches from dead. I'm at a loss, Jack. I knew MacGraths were crazy, but I didn't know they were masochists."

"I'm not a masochist." Well, not really. Though if he thought back over the last few years, he could probably find a handful of antics to support her idea. "I simply don't have a choice on how I live anymore. I'm ruled by something completely different."

"Drugs?" She spun, planting her hands on her hips. "That's it, isn't it?"

"I'm not on drugs." Checking to make sure he had something on beneath the sheets, Jack set his feet on the floor and stood. He tightened the drawstring of his black pajama pants and steadied himself on the bedpost. Branson must've changed him, thank goodness. His muscles were sore from the fight, but he had energy in him. A blessing in disguise. "I'm on adrenaline."

"I don't understand."

He teetered between the urge to tell her everything—the

whole, tragic truth—and the fear that she'd run. If she did take off, he'd be dead before summer, he was sure of it.

But if there was a chance that she might complete the Luminary bond with him, and save him...

He had to try.

Stretching and flexing to assess the damage, he strode closer. Isabelle's gaze homed in on his bare chest, his abs, and then his lips. Her eyes went wide, as if she thought he was coming in close to kiss her. Oh, but didn't he wish.

"I'm 320 years old, and have yet to find my mate." His voice turned darker, graver than he'd meant. "Two decades ago, my health took a turn for the worse. I wasn't expected to survive the year. A wolf pack medicine man told me the tale of unmated wolves living off of adrenaline rushes. He said the surge of the chemical in my bloodstream would elongate my life, though he couldn't say for sure how long."

Squinting, Isabelle rubbed her temples. "So you're..."

"Dying, Isabelle."

She stood still as stone. "Oh," she said.

As if she understood. But she couldn't possibly.

"At first, it only took something startling to get the blood pumping through my veins. But now, I'm getting used to the adrenaline. The thrills are wearing off. It's taking extreme measures to keep my body functioning day to day."

"So the helicopter—"

"The fights—"

"The whole *drive like a bat out of hell* being just what you needed—"

"All that is a normal part of my life. I have to find new things like that every day. The only thing that can save me for good is finding and bonding with my fated mate...you."

Mouth gaping, her gaze shifted around the room as if she were searching for something that made sense. But there were no answers in the woodwork. He'd looked a thousand times over.

"I'm so sorry, Jack," she said, her voice solemn. "I wouldn't wish that on my worst enemy. How much longer do you think you have?"

He swallowed down the spoiled truth. "There's no way to tell. Sometimes I feel myself slipping, but I've already lived twenty years past my expiration, so who knows? Could be another month, another year, or seven hundred. It all depends…"

"Whoa, whoa, rewind." She put her hands up in the space between them. "And you think *I'm* your Luminary? The one who's going to extend your life? I told you before, you're wrong. You should stop wasting your precious time with me and use it to find your real Luminary."

"No time with you is wasted."

"Would you stop that?" She pushed him away, though she lacked the force and the conviction in her touch. "You're a MacGrath, I'm a Connelly. There's no way fate would put us together, across the world from each other, from two packs that hate each other. My father doesn't just dislike your family, Jack. He loathes every one of you for the crimes you committed when werewolves first immigrated here."

The sting of dishonor pinched his side. "I know what my family did in the past, but that wasn't me. I've lived my life differently. With honor."

"Still, he resents everyone who bears the MacGrath name. There is no way we're a perfect match."

"You're it for me, Isabelle," he said, and took her hands. They were soft and warm, molding into his perfectly. She didn't pull away. "And I don't think you're my Luminary, I know you are. I can feel it here." Slowly, he guided her hands to cover his heart. From the closeness, his heart sped, feeding electric impulses of need through his veins. "Don't you feel *anything*?"

"I…" Her eyes fluttered closed. "…I feel your heart beating against my palm, and I can sense the lust racing through you, but that's all it is. Lust. The Luminary bond is so much more than that."

"We have more."

"You can tell me that until you're blue in the face, but I don't feel it."

"Then let me show you."

Tunneling his hand through her hair to the back of her neck, Jack dragged her against him. She gasped in shock, her eyes wide as his lips crushed against hers. Fire burst through him at the contact, but he kissed her slowly. A simmering burn she should've felt in her toes.

Her lips were firm. Unyielding.

As he loosened the hold on her neck and teased her hair through his fingers, he picked up the scent of her arousal. Sweet and unmistakable. She slanted her mouth over his— the tiniest movement—and then opened up on a soft, panting moan. Slipping his tongue past her lips, he teased her with it. Unwound her with the skill of his mouth.

He was in complete control—where he liked to be.

Shivers of lust rattled through him as she explored his mouth with long, luscious strokes of her tongue. She nipped at him. Sucked and drew his bottom lip into her mouth. And just like that, he surrendered.

• • •

Jack may've been deceitful by blood and a liar by nature, but hot damn holy honeysuckle, he knew how to kiss. From the moment his lips touched hers, flames of desire licked through her. Her body flashed hot, melting the bitterness she'd been harboring.

Still, her father's voice rang in her ears.

Never trust a MacGrath.

Was Jack really weakening? Was all that adrenaline mumbo-jumbo the truth? She wanted to believe him, but could she?

"Jack," she mumbled against his lips. Her knees wobbled as the floor disappeared beneath her feet. "What are you doing to me?"

"Showing you how good we could be together."

Grabbing a handful of her hair, he urged her head back and brushed his lips down her throat. She wrapped her arms around his neck, hauling herself against him as his mouth slid along her skin. Every nerve ending in her body awakened. Hunger speared through her. And as he pulled her face down to his and kissed her, passion flared deep in her belly.

This time, when her lips met his, primal need surged through her. She wanted him hovering over her as their hips pressed together. Craved the pressure of his body as he drove deep inside her. Gripping need snaked through her until she was panting into his mouth and clawing her hands up and down his back.

"Ahem," a voice said from the doorway. "Mr. MacGrath?"

Branson stood in the doorway, his hands clasped in front of him.

Peeling her body from his, Isabelle jumped back and rubbed her tingly lips. Now that she was free from his bizarre magnetism, his words rang in her ears.

I'm dying...

"Branson, your timing is impeccable." Jack snatched the pillow off the chair beside them and covered his groin. "Whatever it is, it can wait another six hours. Come back then."

Six hours?

Is that how long she'd be in his bed?

Shivers danced over her skin at the thought.

No, she shouldn't be feeling lust and craving his seduction. She should be concerned about his health…shouldn't she?

"Sir, this is urgent," Branson pressed as stress lines formed at his eyes. "The painting you…have planned to *purchase* from the Grady brothers is here, but they're… Sir, if you would come out and meet them, you could—"

"Spit it out," Jack growled.

"They've changed the price, sir. They want more money for their…efforts."

Why did it seem as if he was talking in code? Tiptoeing around what he really wanted to say?

"They're in your office," he went on, "and refuse to leave until you pay them what they ask."

Sighing, Jack scrubbed his hands through his hair. "Couldn't have come at a worse time."

"What's going on?" Isabelle asked.

"It's nothing for you to worry about. It's only a snag." He brushed her arms as if he'd done it a hundred times before. His hands felt oddly natural on her body. They felt right. "Branson, tell them I'll be right there."

Branson nodded, leaving them alone. Moments ago, when their bodies were pressed together, she was in tune with every beat of Jack's heart, every breath of air escaping his lungs, every desire in his body. But now, it was gone, leaving her cold.

His chilling words haunted her mind.

I'm dying.

"Listen," Jack said, comforting her with the intensity of his gaze. "There's nothing I'd like more than to continue this with you, but the Grady brothers won't wait, and this is important."

More important than living in this moment and taking me to bed? She scratched the thought from her head.

"How long will you be?" she asked, unable to ignore the desperation flooding through her. She wanted his lips over hers again, his tongue sweeping against her cheek, and that delicious warmth blooming through her.

"Why?" His eyebrows pinched together. "Do you have to be somewhere?"

Your bed.

No, that wasn't right. She shouldn't be thinking such things.

But even if she did have plans to head back to Ireland, she'd be so damned distracted by the memory of his mouth, she wouldn't be able to function. There was something in his kiss she couldn't put behind her. Heat and power, and…the promise of more. She couldn't deny it, and wanted—*needed*—to figure out what was happening.

Two seconds ago, she hadn't particularly liked him.

Now, though…

Licking her bottom lip, she tried to savor the tantalizing taste of him. It stirred something inside her chest, warming her through.

There was only one way she was going to shake him. They had to go out. Explore the connection sparking between them. Then, when she tired of him, when she learned everything horrible thing about his past, she could leave San Francisco and never look back. Never think about Jack MacGrath again.

"I don't have plans." Anxiety rippled through her like a cold wave. "But since we didn't get to finish our date last night, I thought maybe you might like the chance to do something. If you're feeling up to it, that is."

The corners of his lips curled into a heart-stopping smile. "So it was a date."

She fought the urge to leap into his arms and plant her mouth on his again. Kiss that smile right off. Shock him and thrill her at the same time.

What the hell was happening to her?

One taste of Jack's mouth and her system had gone

haywire.

"Do you feel good enough to go out or not?" she blurted.

"Nothing could keep me from taking you out." His hands found her waist, and he gripped softly. "Name the place. Anywhere in the world."

But she liked right where she was…

"Okay." She gazed up into his smoky-brown eyes and tingled all over. "Go take care of business with the Grady brothers, and we'll finish what we started."

And then she'd know, once and for all, if their connection was based on lust or something deeper.

Chapter Nine

Jack didn't say anything to the Grady brothers at first.

He knew better than to come into the office swinging. Instead, he leaned back in his plush office chair, tented his fingers together, and waited.

Micah Grady—the twitchy brother with the short fuse—leaned across Jack's desk, pointing a fat finger toward his chest. "It occurred to us, while we were making our way out of Switzerland, that this painting is worth much more than two hundred million. I think it might be in your best interest to make another offer."

Jack's gaze flipped between the werewolf brothers. They were identical twins with short, dark hair, beady eyes, and biceps that could choke a man out in two seconds flat... and probably had. They weren't exactly the same, though. A century of working with them had told Jack that much. Micah was the talker with the temper, but Solomon was the Grady to watch out for. The guy didn't speak much. But when he did, you listened, or you ended up on Channel Ten news as the next John Doe getting pulled out of the bay.

"I thought my offer was more than fair," Jack said, removing the briefcase from beneath his desk. "You couldn't pick up any more for it at auction."

"Ah, but we're not at an auction." Micah kinked his neck to the side and gave it a stiff pop. "We've got a private buyer right here. Willing to do anything so that we don't take him to the cops."

Still, no adrenaline rush. Any other morning, he might've had a pulse of exhilaration at the mention of the police bursting down his door. Today, nothing.

"Who said anything about cops?" Jack asked, dropping the briefcase on his desk and spinning it around. "We're talking business here, and I haven't done anything illegal."

From behind his brother, Solomon pulled his cell phone out of his breast pocket. He punched a few numbers onto the screen and spun it around to face Jack.

"Do what you have to do to get the Van Gogh," Jack heard his voice say from the recording. "If you're on board, I'll send over the address where you can find it."

"We going into a museum?" Micah's voice played back.

"No," Jack said. "This guy stole it from a display in Switzerland. You're going to steal it from him."

Micah puffed on a cigar, blowing into the receiver. "And what do you want with it?"

"Leave that to me."

After a long pause, Micah barked, "Our take?"

"Two hundred." *Million*, he'd meant. "Unmarked U.S. currency. It's the last job I'll have you do."

"You retiring, Jackie?"

"Something like that," Jack said, before Solomon hit the stop button.

"The recording alone could put you away, but when they find the painting in your private collection…" Micah whistled. "The case will be as black and white as that painting over there."

Van Gogh's grayscale painting was exquisite, and had been missing from its display for two years. Jack intended to return it—what he'd done to every stolen piece in the last hundred years. He appreciated art too much to stand by while thieves stole it for their private collections. He had a private gallery, too, but he regularly donated the pieces to museums for others to experience and admire.

"How much do you want, Micah?" Jack asked, nodding for Branson to bring over the other briefcases.

"Five." Solomon answered instead, his voice a gravelly rasp. "We want five."

"Whew. Five-hundred-million." Shaking his head, Jack let out a low curse. "You've never asked for a number that high before."

"We never got the feeling you were going out of business before," Micah said, grinning slyly. "What do you say? Five-hundred and we have a deal? Or we take your two hundred for the trouble, *and* sell this hot piece of art to another buyer?"

From outside the office door, footsteps shifted the floorboards. They creaked under someone's weight. Jack nodded in the direction of the door for Branson to check it out. As he pulled it open, though, Isabelle stood in the doorway, a puzzled look on her face. And those damn hideous slippers were still on her feet.

From the hard glare in her eyes, he knew she'd heard part of their conversation. The question was, how much.

"Ms. Connelly, why don't you wait in the back room? Branson will bring you coffee." Trying to hide his knee-jerk reaction to her, Jack motioned for Branson. "I'll be with you in a moment."

"No need to be rude," Micah said, moving to the door and opening it wide for her to pass through. "Aren't you going to introduce us to your new friend?"

Oh, shit.

"I'm Isabelle Connelly." She stuck out her hand. "And you are?"

"You can call me Micah," he said, turning over her hand and kissing the back.

A low rumbling sound erupted from Jack's chest.

"And this is my brother Solomon," Micah continued. Solomon stared, his arms folded over his chest. "We're business partners of Jack's."

"Oh yeah? What kind of business partners?"

For the first time in days, dread weighed heavy on Jack's shoulders.

She should've stayed in his bedroom. She shouldn't have introduced herself to them…now she was on their radar. For her own safety, it was the last place he wanted her to be.

"Deal." Desperation streaking through him, Jack stood from behind his desk. "You hear me, Micah? I'll get you what you ask by the end of the business day."

Two pairs of Grady eyes snapped his way.

"Glad to hear it." Micah grabbed two of the briefcases Branson had brought over and marched toward the door leading to the foyer. Solomon grabbed the handle of the last one in his chubby hand and met his brother at the door. "I really hope you don't retire. For everyone's sake." His sinister gaze took Isabelle in, starting at her angelic face, dropping down her luscious curves, and ending at her feet. "Nice slippers, Cinderella."

And then they walked out, leaving their stench behind. When the door clicked shut, Isabelle turned to him.

"Who were those guys?" she asked innocently.

He knew her well enough to know there was an undercurrent of accusation in her tone.

"How much did you hear?"

"You just bought that Van Gogh for five-hundred-million."

He nodded, striding toward the painting. "Anything else?"

"They said it was hot." She tapped her fuzzy-slippered foot against the hardwood floor. It was hard to be stern-faced with someone who wore pink mops on her feet. "I've never been good at math, but one plus one equals a stolen painting in your office." She shook her head and glowered. "You know, for a second I thought you were actually one of the good guys. I stood in your bedroom thinking how this was crazy that I was starting to feel— You know what, all that matters is that my father warned me not to trust a MacGrath. I should've believed him. You stole that painting—who knows how many others?"

It was disheartening how eager she was to doubt him. All because of the lying and cheating his ancestors had done hundreds of years before they met.

Clutching the work in his cold hands, Jack stood and faced her. "I didn't steal a thing."

"Okay, so you hired the Goon brothers to do it for you."

"Grady."

"Whatever." She charged at him and tried to rip the painting from his grasp. "Same difference. Whether *you* stole it or they stole it *for* you—"

"It was already stolen." He tightened his grip. "They simply stole it back."

She gawked, yanking harder. "That painting belongs in a museum."

"Exactly."

As if on cue, Branson swept through the door leading to the foyer. "Sir, the curator is here to see you. Are you ready, or should I have her wait?"

Hands freezing on the canvas, Isabelle narrowed her eyes at him. "Curator?"

"For the museum where the art was stolen," Jack said

simply, meeting her stare over the top of the canvas. "She's here to pick it up and return it to its proper place."

"But..." Isabelle glanced at Branson, who stood in the doorway looking unamused by the tug-of-war over the Van Gogh. "You already have someone here to pick it up? You stole it—er, bought it. They were just here."

Maybe she hadn't heard him.

"Time is a luxury that's been denied to me." Jack loosened his grip on the painting, and then let her have it. "I have to make sure things move quickly, or they might not happen at all."

Her lips parted, ever so slightly, as if having her mouth open helped her think. But the second the curator strode into the room—fair skin, platinum-blond hair, and legs for days—she clamped her mouth shut.

"Let me see it," Ms. Sorensen crooned, taking out a pair of thin-rimmed glasses from her bag. "I've been waiting too long."

Isabelle turned, holding up the art, but didn't say a word.

"It's just as striking as I remember." Ms. Sorensen held out her hands. "May I?"

Nodding, Isabelle handed it over and backed toward Jack's desk. Ms. Sorensen analyzed the frame, the smudges in the corners, and the canvas itself. As if it passed her inspection, she grinned wide.

"I'm thrilled it'll be going home," Jack said, shoving his hands in his pockets. "Might I suggest you amp up security to take better care of it this time?"

Ms. Sorensen couldn't tear her studious eyes away from the painting. "Oh, you better believe it. We can't thank you enough, Mr. MacGrath."

As the curator swept out of his office, Jack turned to Isabelle. She leaned back against his desk, staring at the ground and shaking her head, as if trying to process something that was too difficult. Was he finally getting through to her? If anything could change Isabelle's opinion of him, it had to be this. With the curator returning the painting to its proper home, Isabelle had to know he wasn't anything like his thieving ancestors.

"Penny for your thoughts?" he asked.

"Yeah." She huffed into a nervous laugh. "Five hundred million of them."

Chapter Ten

A little after noon, Jack led Isabelle to his bike, which had been parked alongside his house. It was black and rugged. Wide tires. Bulky engine. Narrow passenger seat on the back. Swinging his leg over, he mounted the bike and handed Isabelle a helmet.

"Are you sure you're okay? I mean, after the fight last night—"

"I appreciate your concern," he interrupted. "But I told you, I'm fine."

He certainly looked *fine*. He'd changed into dark-washed jeans, a cotton T-shirt, and a black leather jacket. She'd never had a thing for bikers before, but he nailed the viciously sexy facade. And from the warmth blooming between her legs, he could've nailed her, too. Right here, right now.

It was a good thing Branson had brought her bag from the Hyatt to Jack's place; she was prepared for the ride. While she'd packed light for her trip, she had jeans, a couple cute long-sleeved shirts, and a warm coat. Everything she needed. Except a better defense against Jack's charm, apparently.

"What is this thing?" she asked, gawking at the bike.

"It's a Ducati." He brought it roaring to life, vibrating the cement beneath her feet. "And my favorite way to see the city."

Nerves flitted through her as she took the helmet and shoved it on. "It's a monster. Why can't we take my Camry?"

"The Camry isn't nearly as fun."

True, but… "This is going to give me helmet head."

"Your head is gorgeous, whatever shape it's in." Laughing, he turned and tightened the strap beneath her chin. "Well, I didn't think it was possible for anyone to look adorable in this. But you"—he adjusted it over her head—"pull it off."

Okay, so she might've felt a little better about this whole thing.

"Hop on," he said, putting on his own helmet. "And hold tight."

That she could totally do. It seemed as if from the moment they kissed, a switch had flipped. Her body craved being near his. She shivered with excitement from the mere thought of holding him tightly as they zipped through the city.

Blowing out a shaky breath, Isabelle gripped his shoulders as she straddled the bike and situated herself over the back. Teetering on the seat, she slipped her hands around Jack's waist and hugged her body against his. Heat radiated through his leather coat, right into her chest, instantly relaxing her.

This was what she'd needed all along. In his bedroom, his office, on the back of a monster bike…whatever. Didn't matter.

She breathed him in. Even through the leather, she could pick up his intoxicating scent. It rumbled through her, filling her with a light, airy kind of happiness she'd never felt before.

"You ready?" he asked, easing the bike down the drive.

As she nodded, he shifted gears. The engine growled like a wild animal. With a squeal, she tightened her grip around his waist and buried her face in his back. But within a few seconds, the wind whipped around them, bringing with it the interesting scents of the city. Salt from the bay. Clam chowder wafting from somewhere nearby. Car exhaust. Peeking through fluttering lids, Isabelle took in the passing cityscape.

"Lombard Street." Jack pointed left, and they turned, taking a sudden dip. The road was paved with brick and impossibly steep. One hairpin turn led to another. They zigzagged one way before immediately curving the other.

"It's famous for being the crookedest street in the world," Jack said, turning his head so she could hear him.

"Yeah." She leaned closer. As tight as she could get. "I see why."

Grinning ear to ear, she took in the fragrant hydrangeas blooming alongside the narrow road. Studied the architecture of the houses looming over the street. The whole scene was stunningly beautiful in its uniqueness.

"That was crazy," she said as they slowly wound down to the bottom. "I've never seen anything like that before."

"Just wait." Throttling back, Jack sped through the city, one light after another, rumbling the whole way. "You're going to love this ride."

He took her through the colorful neighborhood of Haight-Ashbury, drove around charming Union Square and the crowded Mission. He pointed out everything like a competent tour guide—as if he read her mind and her heart. She'd wished to see the highlights of the city while she was here, but hadn't had time for it. She'd mentioned her desire briefly when they were in the de Young, but hadn't expected him to remember.

He really was attentive. Would he be that way as a lover? Aware of every heightened nerve as she crested toward climax?

Damn it, how had one kiss made her hyperaware of how

sensual he was?

It was as if she'd woken up from some kind of a sexual slumber.

While she loved every minute of their ride and the delicious tingling in her middle, there were things she wanted to talk to him about. The painting he'd returned to Switzerland. His predicament with adrenaline rushes, and how quickly he was weakening. And why their kiss made her want to do naughty things, despite the fact that she knew she shouldn't.

As if he read her mind, he veered into a parking area near Pier 15. Pulling the motorcycle into a private section of the public lot, Jack turned off the engine and waited for her to dismount before getting off the bike himself.

"What do you think of my city?" he asked, setting their helmets on his bike.

"It's breathtaking." She was still reeling as she fluffed life back into her hair. "I didn't think I'd be able to experience everything in such a short amount of time."

"Oh, you haven't seen anything yet." He grinned, shooting her that smile she liked so much. "I find that if you step back, away from the drama and noise, you can easily grasp the whole picture. You can appreciate the simple beauty of things…and remember not everything is as complicated as it seems when you're in the middle of it."

As he said the last words, his voice deepened to a sexy rumble.

Not everything is as complicated as it seems.

Like what was happening between them? She wondered. Is that what he'd meant? Oh, but if he only knew…

"Come on," he said, and took her hand. His touch was warm and gentle, guiding her toward a massive silver yacht moored to the dock. It was luxurious and sleek. The most beautiful boat she'd ever seen. Three stories, from what she could tell, with an open area on top to lounge.

He took her hand as it rested at her side. "All aboard, Miss Connelly."

"This is yours?"

"I like being out on the sea. It's calming."

He pulled her toward the ship as she picked her jaw off the floor. She'd been on a few boats in her life, but nothing like this. It was beyond elegant. Over the top.

"It was the fastest yacht I could find on the market at the time," he said as they stepped on board. "Powerful, too."

"Of course it is." She glanced at him out of the corner of her eye. "Because you need the rush, right?"

Nodding slowly, he led her up a narrow set of stairs to the upper deck. It was even more gorgeous up close. The whole ship was decorated in white and black, from the shiny flooring to the lounge cushions to the glass of the bar along the far side.

"Do you take this out often?" she asked.

"Not as much as I'd like, but it's quiet on the water. A good place to reflect on what's important."

Yeah, she bet.

As she stood against the rail near the front of the ship, the crisp ocean wind rushed through her hair, and the floor trembled beneath her feet. She felt refreshed up here. Free, somehow. Being with Jack was an adventure like nothing else. It seemed as if she was always guessing with him. Constantly being taken on a wild ride. She'd only been in San Francisco for three days, and she'd already been to a museum, an underground werewolf fight club, wine country, and now this. And so much had changed within her, too. Last weekend, she hated anyone with the name MacGrath. Saturday and Sunday, she was intrigued, despite herself. And now, if she wasn't careful, she might beg him to kiss her again.

"Where are we headed, Captain?"

"Oh, I'm not the captain." The boat pulled away from the

dock and headed into the bay. "At least not today."

On the shoreline, skyscrapers seemed to rise against the edge of the sea, before a backdrop of pristinely blue sky and rolling hills. And in the forefront, a giant Ghirardelli sign hung high, visible to passing boats in the bay.

"If it's all right with you," he said, standing beside her, "we're going to head out into the bay, sail around Angel Island, Alcatraz, and then maybe sweep under the Golden Gate."

"Whatever you want. I'm along for the ride." Leaning over the rail as they headed out, she sighed. "So…how did you get involved with the black-and-white Van Gogh? The one in your office?"

"Ah, another game of twenty questions." He clasped his hands together as he leaned over the rail next to her. "When I heard it was stolen from the museum in Switzerland, I hired the Grady brothers to get it back."

"Do you have an investment in it?"

"No."

"Then why spend so much money to get it back?" She frowned as she gazed out over the boxy white building in the center of Alcatraz. "Why get involved with people like the Gradys knowing full well how bad it would look if they got caught and ratted you out? I mean, you could've ended up someplace like this."

"Then it's a good thing the prison's been shut down for fifty-some-odd years." He chuckled tightly. "I will admit the Gradys are not my favorite people to work with, but they get the job done. They've never failed an assignment I've given them. To date, they've returned thirty stolen works from museums around the world."

She snapped her gaze his way. Only he wouldn't look at her. "You've recovered thirty stolen pieces?"

He nodded, only once, and then slowly turned his head to

meet her gaze. "It's not something I like to advertise."

She huffed into a laugh. "Why the hell not? It's better than people thinking you're an art thief."

People like her father, for one.

"I'd rather keep my hobbies to myself. The curators I've worked with know what I do, and they know where to find me if something comes up. But I've asked them to keep my contributions quiet." As they sailed toward Angel Island, Jack said, "On a clear day like today, you can see Napa from there."

Nice change of subject…

"Really?"

He nodded and stole behind her. Resting his hands on the rail, he trapped her body with his. Rested his cheek next to hers as he peered out over the horizon. The air around them charged with intensity as the heat from his chest radiated into her back. She bloomed with desire. Leaned back against him and bit back a soft sigh.

"There." He pointed in the distance. "Can you see it?"

No, but she could *feel* it.

She wanted to spin in his arms. Look up into his sultry brown eyes. Kiss those lips until she was drunk on the heady taste of him.

"Isabelle?"

"Hmm?" She hadn't realized he was waiting for an answer. *Shit.* "Oh yeah. I see it."

Rather than release her, he stayed behind her, his chin resting on her shoulder. And she didn't want him to move. Not as long as these tingly feelings were fluttering inside her. Thousands of butterflies released in her chest and beat their tiny wings against her rib cage.

Why was this happening? What had changed when he kissed her?

As they sailed around Angel Island, its grass and rock hills were a spectacular contrast against the urban landscape in the distance. Looking at the rugged countryside, one wouldn't think San Francisco was a short boat ride away. And then it struck her. Looking at Jack's muscular physique, square jaw, and the wide breadth of his shoulders, one would never expect that he was dying inside.

Although she would've liked to stay another couple days to explore what was happening between them, she couldn't. Finding two paintings was a major bonus, but she still had to track down ten others, and it wasn't going to be a picnic. Back home, Neil was searching the auction circuit for information, but last night she'd checked her texts. No luck yet. He'd also said her father was fighting to hang on.

Her heart ached to spend more time with him, to experience more of this life with him at her side. It tore her up inside to see him sick and jaded. She chilled as uncertainty settled over her skin in a clammy wave.

As they approached the Golden Gate Bridge, Jack coiled his arms around her waist. How did he know she craved comfort in this moment more than any other? Even though she'd had a year to come to grips with the fact that her father was dying, she hadn't accepted it. Couldn't recognize the truth. Pain whipped through her, and her eyes burned with tears. Jack held tighter, as if he could feel the agony ripping through her. Turning in his embrace, she stared up at him.

His jaw clenched and unclenched as his hands skated up and down her back. "Do you know it's a San Francisco superstition that you have to kiss when you pass under the Golden Gate or you'll have seven years of bad luck in your love life?"

She blinked back tears. "Really?"

She turned her attention to the bridge as they passed underneath its rusted beams. When she brought her gaze back to center, Jack was staring through her, heating her with the promise of a future she shouldn't want. Her heart sped, and her knees went weak.

"No," he said, smirking with those plush lips. "Not really."

She smacked him playfully in the chest. "You're so full o' blarney."

Moving her back , he pinned her against the rail, robbing the air from her lungs.

"I love when those little idioms come out," he said, so close to her mouth. "Drives me mad."

And then he kissed her. Pressed against her, mouth to mouth, hip to hip. Her stomach tumbled and then caught as the shadow of the bridge passed over them, and the sun's rays hit them on the other side. Tunneling his hands into her hair, he tugged her against him to deepen the kiss. His lips were soft and tender, but the heat was demanding. Scorching and undeniable. His tongue swept inside, questioning her true desire with each brush of her cheek. She answered on a whimpered sigh and threw her arms around his neck.

She didn't know how it was possible, but in one day, she'd seen the best San Francisco had to offer.

"Isabelle," he said against her mouth.

"Mm-hmm?"

He kissed her nose, her cheek, her lips.

"Will you come back to my place? There's something I'd like to show you."

There went those butterflies again.

Maybe she hadn't seen the best of San Francisco yet...

Chapter Eleven

A little before nightfall, they arrived at his house. She had to pick up her things and head to the airport before too long.

Maybe after another kiss. Or four.

"I'd like to thank you for saving my life last night," Jack said, leading Isabelle down the hall. "For letting me taste your lips this morning…and this afternoon." Gently, he caressed her lower lip with his thumb. She shivered at his touch. "There's only one thing I can think to give you that would show you the depth of my appreciation."

Oh yeah? How deep would his "appreciation" go?

Taking Jack's hand, Isabelle let him escort her to a giant door at the end of the hall. "Is this your red room?" she asked, blush creeping into her cheeks. "Because I should tell you now I'm not into it."

"No, I believe Branson said the color he painted on the walls was stone gray." Smirking, Jack turned the handle and pushed the door open wide. "But I like the fact that you're still standing here if that's where you thought I was taking you. Close your eyes." Ever so gently, he brushed his hands down her forehead, so she'd close them. "Step in. That's it."

Although he guided her, she tripped over her own foot and stumbled. He caught her, snaking an arm around her waist.

"Easy," he said, leading her into a room that smelled of white tea and fig. The aroma was luxurious and clean, and if she wasn't mistaken, the temperature took a sudden drop the moment they entered the room. "Before you see the surprise, I want you to know that I appreciate every single item in this room equally."

Okay, now she was *really* intrigued.

Peeking with one eye, Isabelle searched around the spacious room. It wasn't a room at all. It was a gallery. *His* private gallery. The walls were painted deep stone gray, as he'd said. Dim lights shone from the ceiling, illuminating the hanging artwork. There were Monets, Renoirs, Warhols, and—

Hold up.

She strode closer to one piece in particular.

"*Werewolf at the Great Wall*," she breathed, touching the bottom of her painting. She'd painted it fifteen years ago. She could still smell the scent of wood, grass, and earth as it'd surrounded her on that warm summer night. "Where'd you…"

She whirled around, cutting her thought short.

Jack stood in the center of the room, a smug look of satisfaction on his gorgeous face. But it wasn't the vision of him in his gallery that had the breath ripping from her lungs. It was the collection of art on the wall behind him—the collection of Bella Nolan art.

"I…" Her feet moved closer of their own accord as tears stung her eyes. "You…my—the artwork…it's…"

Now she wouldn't have to waste weeks, months, years tracking down her work to display in one place.

Did Jack have any idea how much this meant to her?

Without thinking, she ran into his arms. He caught her, embracing her tightly, nuzzling into her hair.

Her works were all there, with the exception of the very first, of course. *Werewolf in Paris, Werewolf in London, Werewolf in the Outback...*

As Isabelle circled Jack's private gallery, it struck her how foolish she'd been. Her father had been wrong, and she'd believed him wholeheartedly, even when the truth stared her in the face.

Jack wasn't a thief.

His body was banging; he was sharp-witted and smart, and had a mysterious vibe to him that had intrigued her from the start. Judging from the exchange in his office, he was generous, too. And man, could he kiss. He could probably do other things with as much skill.

But that still didn't mean they were fated mates.

As much heat as there was in his kiss, the Luminary spark was more than that. It was a *knowing*. A whisper of claiming and possession deep down in her soul. She hadn't heard it yet.

Despite that, Jack had let her in. He felt comfortable enough with her to tell her about his predicament. He'd taken her to Napa to get another painting, and shown her around his city. He'd been open and honest, revealing his gallery when he could've kept it to himself.

And he didn't know she was the one who'd created them all.

That needed to be remedied.

She stood in front of *Werewolf in Moscow*. Admired Saint Basil's Cathedral and its brightly colored domes. Brushed her hands over the Northern Lights in the background and the werewolf standing impressively in front of it all.

"I can't believe you have all of these," she mumbled, stroking them each as she passed by. "Was Jasmine right? Did you start collecting when you'd given up hope of finding your

Luminary?"

Jack wandered through the gallery behind her, his hands shoved into his pockets. She'd noticed he did that when they shook.

"I'm not sure which came first, but she was on target. The work speaks to me. There is a softness to the strokes of the brush that contrasts the sharpness of the urban landscape. And the wolf in those settings…brilliant. I've dreamed of being in each of those places in wolf form."

Interesting.

He'd revealed his collection, making her dream of showing her father all of her artwork a very real possibility.

She'd give him something in return—something to remember her by.

"More than that," he said, coming to stand beside her, "when I study the art, an odd thrill shoots through me. It's like an adrenaline rush, but different. It's electric, if that makes any sense."

It made total sense; she had the same feeling when they kissed.

"Jack," she said, turning to him. "I have to tell you something. And it's something that not many people know."

"All right." His dark eyes glistened with uncertainty. "Shoot."

She paused, looking at each of the pieces of art in turn. She'd never actually told anyone this. In every other case— and there were very few cases to begin with—she'd been discovered when she'd put out the call for werewolf models or been caught in the act by another member of the pack.

Nerves rattled through her and gathered in her stomach.

She took a deep breath and said, "I'm Bella Nolan."

Frowning, he took a step back. "What do you mean?"

"I mean," she said, spreading her arms wide, "I painted all of these. *Werewolf in Manhattan, Moscow, Outback, Paris—*

all of them."

He stared, disbelieving, unmoving.

"I started painting years ago, and was proud of what I was creating. My first painting, *Werewolf in Dublin*, was of my father in wolf form, standing in front of Saint Patrick's Cathedral. It wasn't drawn from life, but from a memory I have when I was young, at my mother's funeral." Her throat ached, stinging with the sudden threat of tears. "I showed him, and he—he destroyed it. He ordered me to stop painting, to focus more on pack matters. I couldn't quit though, not after I had the bug. So to hide it from him and the pack, I continued under a false name, to keep my true identity secret."

Jack's hands found her shoulders. "You're Bella Nolan?"

His hands were calm and steady. Now it was her turn to shake.

As she trembled full force, he wrapped her up and brushed his hands down her hair, soothing her. "I can't believe it...why didn't you tell me sooner?"

"I've never actually told anyone before," she whispered, her head resting against his chest. His heartbeat drummed against her cheek, calling to something deep within her. "It was harder than I thought it'd be to admit it, I guess."

"How could your father not appreciate this part of you?"

She shrugged. "I'm collecting the art for him, to hopefully make him proud. I'm going to display it in one place so that he can understand the gravity of it. To truly comprehend that it's not just a hobby, but a deep-rooted part of me."

"He'll realize it. Maybe all he needed was time."

Now for the most important question of all...

"Will you sell them to me?" She slowly bent into him as his hand stilled on the small of her back. "I'd pay well more than they're worth, of course."

He exhaled heavily, though he didn't let her go. He held tight. And then shuddered against her.

"I can't sell them. I'm sorry but I can't, not when I know you're leaving me." As her heart dropped, he said, "I understand that you need them to show your father and I won't deny you. You're more than welcome to borrow them—I'll even have Branson load them onto my jet for you to take when you go home. You have my warmest blessing to display them all in Dublin." He went solid as stone in her arms. "As long as you promise to personally return them when you're finished."

Borrowing them wasn't what she wanted, but it *did* give her a reason to come back to him.

"You really want me to come back and pester you some more?" she whispered as he nipped at her earlobe.

"I want you here with me like this, every single day"—his breath was hot and moist on her neck, and tingling her down to her toes—"for as long as you'll have me."

"Well not right *here*, per se." She spun in his embrace and threw her arms around his neck. "We'd get hungry eventually."

He smirked. "That's what Branson is for." And then he kissed her, melting her all over again. "If you'd only stay with me…"

Focus. Why was it so difficult to think straight around him?

Lust was different from love—she'd be wise to remember it.

For the first time since she met him, she wished—with a tiny, secret part of her heart—that she was the one for him.

She pulled back, despite herself, and looked him square in the eye. "Thank you for the offer to take the paintings to Dublin. I accept."

Under the circumstances, it seemed like the only way she would be able to show her father at all. And maybe, if one of the paintings really spoke to him, she could make Jack an offer for that one in particular.

This could work…

As Jack's hands skated up and down her back, they began to tremble. "How long will you be gone?" Suddenly his voice was tight. "A week? Two?"

There was no way to know. "I'm not sure."

"Why do you have to go now? What's the rush? Why can't you wait a week, or a month, or whatever makes you comfortable? You could stay with me, if you wanted."

He wanted more time to try to convince her of his feelings. To see if she'd come around and realize that she was, in fact, his Luminary. His motives were transparent. But it simply didn't work that way.

Fated mates *knew* they were. It was a calling in their core. A primal instinct to possess the other.

"Jack…" How to say the words that hurt her the most? Merely thinking about them made her head dizzy with fear. "My father is dying. He has cancer." The words tasted bitter and rotten, burned her tongue, and carved a big ugly hole out of her heart. "He doesn't have long left. What I'm doing—the art I'm collecting—it's my last chance to get him to understand how much this means to me. How much I want it to mean to him." Her stomach turned, aching as if she'd been speared, all the way through. "I think it could bring us together in his final days."

"I'm so sorry, Isabelle." He kissed her forehead, slow and loving. "So sorry. I've lost both my parents, all the family I ever had really, so I completely understand what you're going through. Whatever you need—"

"You've already given it to me," she said, turning her attention to the paintings. "This is what I wanted. I wasn't sure I'd find all the paintings in time, and I wasn't even sure how much I'd have to start with. You helped make my dream come true."

Which was the reason she couldn't leave him empty-handed. Completely rob him of his favorite pieces without so much as a thank-you. There was one way to thank him for what he'd done, what he'd given her.

"You were kind enough to show me the gallery," she said, "and made me happier than I think you realize. I'd like to give you something in return. Something for you to remember me by."

His expression pulled into a frown. "You say that as if you're never coming back."

"No, I'll return to the city." *I'll return to you.* She'd almost said it accidentally. Thank goodness she caught herself. "But I can't strip these off your walls without replacing them with something."

"What did you have in mind?"

. . .

Just after three o'clock in the morning, Isabelle stood at the Golden Gate overlook, where three major park trails converged in a wooded area of the Presidio. She was all business, a clipboard and makeshift easel tucked under her arm. Once she told him of her plans to paint him, he'd sent Branson out to pick up all the supplies she needed.

"This place is remarkable," Isabelle said, staring up at the moon peeking between the trees. "The trails and trees, the Golden Gate in the distance. The lights on the bridge are luminous, aren't they? Shining like stars. It's the perfect place to paint you."

"We shouldn't be bothered here, at least not for a few hours." Nerves pinballed through Jack's stomach. "How long does this usually take?"

"Anywhere from one to five hours, though this canvas is eight by ten so it shouldn't take me as long as a few of the others." She went to work setting up. "The light changes fast, so within two hours it'll look like a completely different painting. I'm going to try to finish before that happens."

"You're amazing," he said, standing with the Golden Gate behind him. "You know that?"

She grinned, and the moonlight illuminated her face in a pearly-white glow. "Let's see how the painting turns out before you call me that."

But he'd called her amazing for many more reasons than the painting. She was giving him something special, a gift he'd cherish for the rest of his life. If only he could say with certainty how long that would be.

Somewhere over the course of the night, hollowness had carved him out. He felt weaker than he had days before. As if tremors were about to rack his whole body. And although being near Isabelle and her artwork was a rush in and of itself, something had changed. The electric currents soaring through him were there, but his hands still shook, and his head still spun.

He didn't have long left.

He could feel the end closing in, and although he refused to admit it to Isabelle, fear had trickled into his chest, paralyzing him. The worse part? She could save him. With the bonding process—vows spoken while they were having sex—his life would be saved.

He'd never felt so close to his goal, yet so far.

Isabelle held his heart—his life—in the palm of her hand. Did she know how important she was to him? Not only because she could save his life, but because she cared enough to do this for him.

As she finished setting up the easel, she stared over the top of her clipboard. "All right. Let's get to it."

Shaking his head as laughter struck him, Jack undressed. No need to burst through his clothes if he didn't have to. He shuffled out of his shirt and flung it to the ground at the base of the nearest tree. He popped the button on his fly. A strangled sound, almost like a whimper, floated on the night breeze. He glanced up, hands on the top ridge of his pants.

Isabelle stared, hunger blazing in her emerald eyes.

"Something I can do for you, Ms. Nolan?"

She shook her head. "No, it's—you're not shy, are you?"

"I don't have any reason to be."

Blushing, she returned her gaze to the clipboard. But her eyes flickered to his bare torso one more time. And then again.

He yanked down his pants, kicked out of them, and then shot one more glance at Isabelle before starting on his boxers. If he wasn't mistaken, she sucked in a clipped breath as he pulled them down and tossed them onto the pile with the others. He couldn't help but flex and twitch his muscles as the warm night air set upon him.

As their eyes met, Jack winked. And then balled all the energy into a pit in the bottom of his stomach. Tendrils of electric currents pulsed through his limbs, making them tingly and warm. And then he shook, head to toe, skin to bone. Muscles elongated, lengthened, and bulked up. With a hearty shake, fur blanketed his body and he dropped to all fours. He fought the urge to howl at the full moon as he completed the shift and sat back on his haunches.

He felt free. Completely exhilarated.

He stretched, bounded around the dirt to get the spring in his legs, and then gazed at Isabelle.

"You're magnificent," she said, her eyes wide. "Your hair…it's black as night. And your eyes…they grab me from here." She paused and dropped the paintbrush to the dirt. Gasping, she bent to pick it up. "It'll make for a beautiful painting." She cleared her throat and narrowed her gaze at the canvas. "Go ahead and pose however feels natural."

Natural would be shifting back to human form, hauling her into his arms, and making love to her right here, right now.

That probably wasn't what she meant.

Instead of doing what he *really* wanted to do, Jack took a wide stance and raised his chin toward the moon. As if he were howling for his mate.

"That's good." With one eyebrow rising in contemplation, she moved her brush over the canvas. "Now don't move."

It was tense at first, holding still for so long. But as the wind blew through his fur and the light around them began to change, something in him changed, too. He relaxed every muscle in his body. Breathed deeply. Felt the fog as it rolled in and coiled around his paws. And then he turned his head, just a little, enough so he could watch Isabelle as she painted him.

She took her art seriously. Glared at the canvas. Struck it with one brush before tossing it aside and choosing another. She swirled colors together, dabbed and splatted. And other times, when passion blazed in her eyes, her wrist would flick gracefully, and a smile would curl her lips.

She truly loved painting.

And he truly loved her.

He hadn't fully realized it before, but now…he was mesmerized watching her this way. Mind, body, and soul, she consumed him. She was his fated mate, but he hadn't realized he could care for her this deeply in such a short amount of time.

"Stop moving," she said, jarring him. "I don't know if you realize this, but every time you look at me you bow your head. It's a tiny movement, but each time it gets lower."

She was right. He hadn't realized it, though the move was exactly the way he felt.

He'd bow down reverently to his queen any day.

"I'm almost finished."

Had the hours really gone by so fast?

Holding still, pretending to howl at the moon, Jack had the realization that this was the last time he'd be with Isabelle for weeks. As soon as she finished the painting, she was taking his private jet back to Ireland. While she painted him, Branson was arranging for all of the artwork to be on board. He was taking her to the airport after this.

Saying good-bye was going to be damn near impossible.

An idea struck. Maybe they didn't have to say good-bye.

He could go to Ireland with her…

Not wanting to ruin the moment by rushing things, he pocketed the thought for later. He'd ask when the time was right.

"Okay." She signed what he assumed was her signature on the bottom corner, and then stood back, admiring her work. "It's finished."

He bounded over, stood beside her, and froze. It was better than anything he could have imagined. There he was, howling at the moon, his stance strong and full of vitality. He didn't look like he was knocking on death's door. No, he looked healthy and solid. Majestic. And behind him rose the two golden towers, their twinkling lights illuminating the night. Between the light and the shadow, the moon and the stars, the strength and the gracefulness…she'd painted her masterpiece.

"I think this is the best one I've ever done." She breathed hard, as if the experience had winded her. "It took so much out of me. More than I thought it would. I feel…invested in it. More than the others."

Eager to touch her, pull her into his arms, and tug her against him, Jack shifted back to human form. Fur smoothed to golden skin. His muscles shortened. His features shifted. And in a few seconds that blurred into one, he stood in front of her. Buck naked.

Her eyes locked on his manhood, and then she gasped, averting her attention to the painting. "You're very, ah—the sun's about to rise—maybe we should go—"

She was beyond adorable when she was nervous.

"Isabelle," he said, cutting her short. "What's the matter?"

"Nothing, nothing at all." She started cleaning up. "We should get out of here as fast as we can. I have a plane to catch. You should take my—your painting. You should take it."

"Isabelle." This time he said her name slowly, tasting every sweet sound of her name. "Look at me."

Nerves spiraled through the air between them. He sensed her hesitation and uncertainty. Although he didn't pick up any hints of fear, something had changed once he shifted back, and she didn't have her feelings in check.

"Isabelle, stop for a second."

This time when he spoke her name, it was a whisper. The softest caress. She finished straightening up, though she stared at the ground and fiddled with her hands.

Why wouldn't she look him in the eye? Had he spooked her somehow?

Slowly, using two of his fingers, Jack tipped her chin toward him. When her eyes met his, they glossed with tears.

"What's wrong?"

She blinked up at him innocently, and his heart hammered against his ribs.

"It's only me, Isabelle."

"I know," she said softly. "That's why I'm flummoxed."

And then she rose up on tiptoe and caught his mouth with hers.

Chapter Twelve

Roping his arms around her waist, Jack hauled her against him. She made a whimpering sound as her feet lifted off the ground, but lost her breath as he crushed his mouth to hers. Any refusal she might've wanted to give him was swallowed by the fierceness of his kiss and the drugging warmth of his body.

"You're a MacGrath," she pushed out as he backed her against the nearest tree. "This is crazy."

"I am a MacGrath." His hands glided over her body, marking her with their heat. "And it feels crazy because it's so right."

Pausing, their eyes met in the dark. Jack's naked body glistened golden tan in the slivers of moonlight peeking through the trees. Muscles flexing in anticipation, he stared. Waiting for her to respond before pressing her further.

"You shouldn't feel like this." She kissed him on a moan, openmouthed and feverish, and clawed her fingers through his hair. "Like your arms belong around my waist…"

He gripped her there, scorching her skin with prickles of

desire.

"Like your mouth belongs on mine…"

He kissed her, slow and fierce, urging her lips apart. Drawing her tongue into a dance with his. And then his mouth slanted over hers, his tongue diving deep. She could sense his hunger and rising need as if they were her own. She was lost in the swirling of his tongue as it explored her mouth. In the wild and honeyed taste of him. In his rich scent as it wafted around them.

"You belong to me," he panted, coming up for air. "And I to you."

She smiled into another kiss, drawing his mouth down over hers with brutal force. Sucking at his bottom lip, she infused him with the smoldering heat burning inside her. Every heightened nerve in her body wanted him. Craved him like no other.

He was everything she shouldn't want.

And everything she needed.

"Take this off"—he licked along her jaw and sucked on her neck—"before I"—he gripped her sweater in his fists and tugged at the bottom—"rip it to shreds."

God, please. Do it.

As if he heard her silent, desperate plea, he yanked off her sweater and flung it to the ground. Reaching around her, he unsnapped her bra and guided it down her quivering arms.

Flesh against burning flesh, he tightened his grip around her waist and moaned. She leaned back, resting on the tree. If it weren't for his hand protecting her, the bark might've scraped her skin. He was cautious and aware, in tune with exactly what she needed.

An unselfish lover.

He kissed her again and went to work on her jeans. Chills scampered down her stomach as her will snapped with the button.

"I have to touch you." He jerked the zipper down. "Now."

Pleasure speared through her as his hands dipped beneath the ridge of her pants and touched tender flesh. He swallowed her soft cries of pleasure with his mouth and stroked her clit. She tugged her against him tighter, craving pressure, needing him closer.

With a gentle nudge, he shoved her pants down around her ankles and widened her stance. She gave him everything he asked, her breath hitching as his hand found her warmth once more.

Lust and insatiable need rippled over his expression as he worked his fingers through her slick folds. As if he knew exactly how to unwind her. He claimed her mouth. Feasted on her lips. Rubbed her where she craved pressure. Sent shock waves of desire undulating through her core.

And then, when he drove a finger inside her, she cried out his name.

"God, Isabelle," he said, his dark eyes blazing with need. "You're so tight."

Stroking her closer and closer to the peak of ecstasy, he held her against him to support her weight. She squirmed in his arms, her legs going weak. And then, when he thrust his tongue into her mouth in time with his fingers, she surrendered. Bucked against his hand. Nipped at his bottom lip. And screamed so loud, her voice echoed into the night.

On a satisfied groan, he withdrew his hand from between her legs and sucked on his fingers. "I'm so hungry for you."

Her legs quivered as the waning pulses of the orgasm lingered in her center. "What about you?"

"We'll get to that." Grinning slyly, he arranged the clothes on the ground into a makeshift bed. And then taking her hand, he laid her down and helped take her pants off the rest of the way. "But I'm not finished with you yet."

Good God.

How much more could she take?

Hovering over her, he supported his weight with his hands planted on either side of her shoulders, creating a cage with his body. His gaze roved over her, though this time it was filled with admiration and awe. He swept a few loose strands of hair out of her face. Brushed his thumb over her bottom lip. And shook his head slowly.

"You're glorious," he said, breathless. "An angel...*my* angel. You might not know it yet, but you came to save me from the dark."

There were no thoughts of correcting him. She *was* his. Something deep in her heart told her so.

As he lowered his head to possess her mouth once more, the heat from his body radiated through hers, burning her up. Primal instincts reared up inside her as his hands glided down her body. Cupped her breasts, and ghosted over her waist. Dipped lower...

This time, his mouth followed the trail of his hands down her body. She went damp as his tongue flicked out over her nipples. First one, then the other.

"I love to hear the little sounds you make when I touch you." He stroked a finger through her heat and groaned. "Will you make the same sounds when I kiss you?"

She shivered as he dived between her legs. He spread them wide with his hands. Gripped her thighs tight. He blew softly over her center, driving her wild. She shook with want. Trembled with deep-rooted desire.

"How bad do you want it?" He swirled his fingers over her thighs, imitating the motions he'd used moments before. And then he pressed a kiss to the dent where her legs met her hips. It was close enough—a taste of what was to come. "Tell me, Isabelle."

She writhed, desperation piercing through her, and grasped his shoulders. "Put your mouth on me."

On a throaty moan, he did as she commanded, dragging his tongue through her heat. She cried out in soul-searing pleasure, her voice strangled as she clawed at his shoulders. He continued his sensual assault, swirling his tongue. Pressing his mouth against her, giving her the pressure she craved. Keeping his lips on her core, his hands slid up her body and kneaded her breasts.

It was too much. Sensation overload.

Without warning, his tongue plunged into her heat. In and out again. She exploded against his mouth, her hips rearing up as the most intense orgasm of her life tore through her. When the blissful convulsions finally ebbed, she went limp. Her vision blurred. Her arms fell to her sides. And when he rose over her, he wore nothing but a sly grin and the largest erection she'd ever seen in her life.

"You're radiant." He planted the softest of kisses on her lips. "Do you know how much I love that I'm the one who gave you that glow?"

How had she been resisting this? They'd wasted the entire weekend at the museum and in Napa when they could've been in his bed. Doing this. Over and over again. And again.

"What are you thinking?" He lay beside her, the evidence of his arousal pressing against her hip. "You frowned just now."

"Nothing." She stroked her hands up and down the ripples of muscle on his stomach, and then gripped the head of his shaft. "I want to pleasure you, too."

"But that wasn't why you frowned." He moaned, laying his head back. "If you were worried about this ending, it doesn't have to, you know."

Yes it did.

She was leaving. Going back to Ireland soon…

And Jack was weakening. He didn't have long left. He'd said so himself. Sure, he looked fine now, full of vigor and stamina, but she'd seen firsthand how his spells could knock him out.

If only she had more time. If only her father weren't sick.

She'd stay in San Francisco for a while. They'd hide out from the world, and cherish the time spent together behind closed doors. She'd help him find his Luminary so that he could live another—

She cut the thought short and worried her bottom lip between her teeth.

The thought of Jack bonding with someone else didn't mesh in her head. It was like trying to argue with herself that the sky was red. Still, if it saved his life, she'd help him find her.

In the distance, the scent of non-shifters hit her nostrils. They both turned in the direction of the aroma—he must've picked it up, too. Down one of the paths leading deeper into the park, a couple strode through the shadows. They were drunk, from the smell of them.

"Come on, we better get out of here. San Francisco has rules about public indecency." Smirking, he helped her off the ground. "Let me take you home, and I'll show you what it could be like if you stayed with me."

If she only had today—a few precious hours—to spend in San Francisco, she wanted nothing more than to be with Jack.

Whatever that meant.

"Lead the way," she said.

• • •

Jack shut his bedroom door and walked Isabelle toward his bed. Disrobing in two seconds flat, he kicked off his shoes. Clothes flew to the corners of the room. Coming at her fast, he peeled the clothes off her body, kissing her silky-soft skin as he went. When she was beautifully nude, standing before him unabashedly, he sucked in a clipped breath. Lush breasts. Soft curves. Milky-white skin, and freckles decorating her cheeks.

She was the perfect combination of sweet and sin. Innocence and irresistible sex appeal.

"Your bed is ginormous." Blushing, she smacked him playfully. "How many women did you plan to have in here at one time?"

"It's not about the number of women I can fit in here"—gripping her waist tight, he hiked her legs around his waist and drove her back, dropping her onto the silk-covered bed—"but what you can do with one woman in it."

Her eyes went wild with excitement as he flipped her over and pulled her down on top of him. Her hair cascaded around her face in a dark, silky waterfall…and he lost his breath.

If he were the artist, he'd paint this moment. Right here.

He pressed a long and languid kiss on her lips, drawing an erotic moan from the back of her throat. It fueled his desire. Reaching up, he cupped her gloriously full breasts in his hands.

"I swear your body was made for me," he said on a groan. "You're so perfect."

She tilted her head to the side and grinned sweetly. "I don't know how you do it, but you make me feel like the most beautiful woman in the world. Like I'm the only one for you."

"You are."

She planted her lips on his and kissed him openmouthed. With passion and promise. As she began to move her hips over his groin—tiny little rocking movements back and forth, back and forth—tendrils of white-hot tension gathered into a ball at the base of his spine.

If he waited another second to feel her heat clench around him, he'd burst.

Thanking God for the fact that werewolves could only get pregnant when the female was in heat, Jack let out a throaty moan. Gripping her hips, he positioned her perfectly over his shaft. He shook. Hovered on the brink of drowning in her slick heat and losing himself completely.

"Jack," she said as she moved over his thick length. "I ache for you."

It was all he needed to hear.

On a hiss, he edged his throbbing tip inside. Wet heat engulfed him, welcoming him deeper. Thrusting slowly, he inched inside her clenching depths. She threw her head back and groaned in pleasure as he finally buried himself to the hilt.

"Isabelle, you feel so"—gripping need pulsed through him as the scent of her arousal hit him—"fucking good. So soft. Tight."

Lifting her hips over him, he guided her in a steady rhythm. Rocking her back and forth. Slowly. And then, when a jolt of lust hit him hard, he flipped her over, pinning her to the mattress. She shrieked in delight, exhilaration and happiness spearing through her. Crossing her arms over her head, he held her in place with one hand and used the other to tease her nipples.

"Oh, Jack…"

He licked and nipped at her lower lip. Drove into her again and again. Passion rising fast, he slid all the way out, and then drove back inside. Pushed back, and plunged in. And then, as he thrust into her core and feasted on the sweetness of her mouth, she cried out. Her depths pulsed, milking him to the brink of his release.

Mine.

• • •

"Jack." She moaned in sheer bliss as he pinned her with his body. He was close—his entire body taut, fighting against the release. "Come inside me."

He rolled his hips against her in a sensual rhythm. Slow

slide out. Deep push in. Grinding against her, he penetrated as far as he could go and demanded more.

Her instincts flared as a fiery current surged inside her.

Mine.

She stilled beneath him.

He matched her, his thrust slowing. "Are you okay?"

Nodding, she urged him down over her again. "I will be when you finally give me what I want."

"There is something so erotic"—he pushed into her, and she arched up. Lowering his head, he sucked her nipple into his mouth—"about a woman who knows how to ask for what she wants."

He sank deeper, stretching her to the fullest. And when she thought he couldn't possibly please her any more, he dipped his hand between their bodies and rubbed her gently. She bucked against him, her head falling back and her mouth dropping open.

Mine.

There was that word again. Echoing in her head. Tugging on something deep in her belly.

"Isabelle, I want to make you mine." He swirled his fingers lightly, right where she craved the pressure. He angled his thrusts so they were shallow…just right…like…that. "Say I can treasure you this way, every day for the rest of our lives."

He wanted to complete the bonding process with her. It would happen now, if it were going to happen at all. They'd press their palms together, make love, and recite vows that would bond them for hundreds of years.

His entire body quaked as he waited for her answer.

Mine.

She was too close to climax. Hovering on the brink.

"Isabelle, look at me."

As his throbbing length filled her with gentle strokes, and his fingers massaged her swollen clit, she gazed up into his eyes. There was lust and raging desire…and love.

Mine.

This time it wasn't her own voice that she heard, but Jack's.

It sent her careering over the edge. The orgasm ripped through her, engulfing her in waves of blinding heat. Her core was still clenching fiercely when he drove into her a second time. And then a third. Sweat trickled down his temple as he thrust harder into her core. His desperate gaze held hers, and on a final, languid thrust, he stilled. His muscles seized. His hips spread her thighs wide. And then he pitched over the edge, filling her with everything he had to give.

My Luminary.

The thought struck her as he collapsed, going limp on top of her. He half supported his weight on his arms and breathed heavily into her hair.

"I knew you'd come around," he mumbled.

"What?"

Rolling beside her, he pulled her against him. "You felt it. You heard my claim in your head, in your heart."

"I feel it now." She nodded, fighting back tears. "I do."

There was no doubting it. He was meant for her, and she for him. Sweet relief rushed through her veins, warming her from the inside out. She'd found her mate. She'd prayed for the day. But on the heels of the primal reaction, waves of trepidation followed, whirling through her like a maelstrom.

"God, Isabelle, I can't tell you how relieved I am. I'd given up hope that I'd ever find you. But from the first moment I met you, not once did I doubt it was you, that you were it for me." He stroked his hand down her shoulder, her arm, to her wrist. "We can be together. Your father will realize we're fated to be one, and he'll have to come around."

"He won't."

Jack spun her to face him and frowned. "Don't tell me that you're…"

The answers were in her eyes—he could see them. He'd have to. She couldn't bond with him. Not until she had her father's approval.

He exhaled heavily. The despairing sound was a knife to the heart.

"If you were going to bond with me, you would've done it when you heard my voice," he said, "when you realized it. It's not going to happen, is it?"

"It will," she said, brushing her hand over his cheek. "But not yet. I just need some time." Time to convince her father that not all MacGrath men were terrible people. "Please don't be mad at me."

"Sweetheart," he said, kissing the tip of her nose. "How could I be mad at you? You're trying to do what's best for your father and your pack. But he must want you to be happy and find the werewolf you're destined to spend the rest of your life with. Don't you think he might change his mind if he knew? Don't you think it's worth the chance?"

She chuckled, though tears threatened. "If he knew I was lying here with you having this conversation, he'd tell me to find someone from our pack to marry, even if it meant shortening my life. Because the role of Alpha comes with the heavy burden of responsibility. It's not about what makes me happy, but what's best for the pack. I've known that was my charge all along, but I never thought I'd actually have to make a decision like this…with someone like you."

"What about in a year or two?" he asked, gazing deep into her eyes. "When your father has passed, and things have calmed down. When you're Alpha, and free to make the rules as you wish. If I'm still…in the picture, would you bond with me then?"

Her stomach wrenched at the thought of losing him. She paused, her thoughts racing through every scenario, every outcome of her actions.

But it wasn't only about her. It was about so many others who would come after her. Although it was easy to focus on the welcoming warmth of Jack's arms, and his steady heartbeat as it thumped against her chest, there was a much bigger picture she needed to focus on.

She needed her father's—the Alpha's—blessing.

"I know that I want to be with you," she said finally.

He smiled as he kissed her. "Then for now, I guess that's all I need to hear."

Chapter Thirteen

A soft beeping sound penetrated Isabelle's dream. In the soundest sleep of her life, she envisioned happily ruling the Irish Wolf Pack with Jack. Hand in hand, heart in heart.

The sound grew louder.

She peeled her eyes open, rolled over, and checked the phone she'd set on the nightstand before they'd fallen asleep.

Neil.

His name flashed across her screen with an alert of the text he'd sent a few minutes before.

Call me. ASAP. It's your dad.

Heart in her throat, Isabelle clutched the phone and slipped out of bed, careful not to wake Jack. She closed the door on her way into the dark hall. Dialed. Prayed her dad was all right.

"Neil," she whispered as soon as her friend answered. "What's happened?"

"He fell in the shower last night. My mum found him and took him to see the doc, but he's not walking and…"

His words trailed off as panic latched onto Isabelle's windpipe, strangling her.

"I'm coming home," she blurted, searching for her shoes. Where had Jack kicked them last night? "Right now."

"The doc says he might only have a week left, maybe two," she heard him say through the fog clouding her brain. "If you wanted to patch things up with him, now's the time."

Lost in a haze, Isabelle circled through the foyer, hand to her head. It was pounding, pinching at her temples. Spots had started forming in front of her eyes.

"I'm on my way."

She was about to hang up when Neil said, "Did you get what you went there for?"

"Yeah." Her gaze skated toward the direction of the gallery. "I got everything I needed."

She winced. When it was worded that way, her relationship with Jack sounded hollow. As if the only reason she was in his home was because she needed the paintings, and not him.

"Good," he said simply. "See you soon."

"Wait…Neil?"

"What is it?"

She paused. *How to say it?* "How do you think my dad would feel if I brought someone back with me?"

"Who—like a male, who?" From the snarkiness in Neil's tone, she could tell he was smiling. "Did you meet someone? Didn't I tell you not to leave your heart in San Francisco?"

"I did meet someone, actually. The thing is, he's a MacGrath."

Silence on the other end of the line.

"Neil?" More silence. "Are you there?"

"What are you thinking, Isabelle?" he said, his tone falling flat. "Are you really going to bring a MacGrath to your dad's bedside? Tell him you fell in love and—"

"I never said I fell in love."

"You wouldn't be asking to bring him home if you didn't love the poor bastard."

Good call. He knew her well.

"It'll kill him, Isabelle," he said softly. "You can't bring him here, not now. This is the worst possible time to tell him he's going to lose his daughter to someone he hates."

She worried her bottom lip between her teeth and nodded in agreement, even though he couldn't see her.

"Okay," she said. "I'm coming home…alone."

"I think that's the right choice. Focus on your dad and the paintings if that's what you want, but the rest will work itself out later. See you soon, Isabelle." And then he ended the call.

Isabelle shuffled toward the gallery. Where the only Bella Nolan painting remaining was the one she'd done of Jack. In front of the Golden Gate. Standing tall and proud.

Rays of morning light spilled through the windows and slanted over the floor in a bright golden glow. Somehow, all the light seemed to focus on the painting—the only one her father would never see.

It was a shame.

It was the best painting she'd ever done. Hands down. And she felt oddly pulled to it—a reaction she didn't have to the others in the collection. Sure, they all meant something, and she had fond memories of creating each one.

But this one in particular…

It showed Jack in the best light. She'd somehow captured the beauty and the grace within him. He wasn't a cruel, deceitful werewolf who took advantage of others at whim as she'd initially believed. As her father still thought.

He was her fated mate. She knew that now.

If she couldn't bring Jack home in the flesh, she could at least talk to her father about him, tell him about the Van Gogh that Jack returned to the Switzerland display, about how he made her feel, about the bond between them.

She could always invite Jack to return to Ireland with her in a few days, after she'd assessed her father's health and buttered him up. Then, when it was safe, her father could meet Jack and witness their connection for himself.

Her father did like to be eased into things, especially ideas that went against what he believed.

The painting would help.

God, she didn't want to take it, but yearned to show it to her father. She would explain things slowly, over the course of a few days. And then, when he finally started to come around to the idea, she'd ask Jack to meet her in Dublin.

The thought struck her, and she instantly ran with it, sliding *Werewolf in San Francisco* off the wall.

As she tiptoed toward his bedroom to ask if he'd mind her taking it, she cracked open the door. He snored. Flipped over on the bed. Flattened out spread-eagled. And then rested his hand on his crotch. All he needed was a good scratching and he'd complete the image of the quintessential rugged male.

"Jack," she whispered, kneeling over the bed. "Wake up. I need to talk to you for a second."

"Pancakes." He grumbled like a big ole bear. "With whipped cream an' blueberries an' syrup. Thank you, miss, I'll have three more."

Smirking, Isabelle gave him a shake. "Jack…"

He didn't move. He was sleeping so deeply. So peacefully. She must've delivered the ultimate knockout punch: love him right, and then lights out.

As she shook him again, harder, her skin prickled with worry. If he opened those gorgeous eyes, would she be able to stare into them and say good-bye? He'd probably draw her into his arms and snuggle against her. Would she be able to pull away and leave his bed? The answer to those questions soured her stomach.

If she wanted to see her father in his final days, she

couldn't wake Jack.

But it'd be okay. She'd make sure of it.

Rather than force him awake, she scribbled a note explaining everything. Her father's fall, and her need to go back and see him. Sleepy orders of pancakes with the works. She'd send for him soon—it wouldn't be long. A few short days. She wasn't abandoning him. She'd be back. They'd figure everything out. She wouldn't let him die.

I must be crazy, but I think I love you.

She scribbled the final words with a smile. He'd be upset that she had to leave this way, but the profession of her love would smooth things over.

On her way out the door with Jack's painting in hand, doubt trickled into her heart. She wasn't doing anything wrong. Not really.

But then why was she feeling this way?

Jack would have to understand.

Of course he would. He loved her. He wouldn't mind if she had to borrow his painting. It wasn't like she was stealing it. He'd meet her in Dublin, and then, when enough time passed, they'd be together. Jack's health had held out this long—well over the three-hundred-year expectancy—so he'd be fine for another couple days. Then, when they bonded, the painting would be *theirs.*

She called a cab at the curb, and then directed the driver to the San Francisco airport, where Jack's private jet was still waiting with the entire Bella Nolan collection.

• • •

Pinching his eyes shut to keep out the morning light, Jack rolled over and swept his hand over the other side of the bed. After their lovemaking last night and the breakthrough they'd had, all he wanted to do was wrap her in his arms and stay in bed all morning. Hell, all day.

But the bed was empty, and the sheets were cold.

Quickly scanning the empty room, he said, "Isabelle?"

His stomach growled violently. And for some reason, pancakes sounded delicious. Pressing the buzzer near the nightstand, Jack waited for Branson's voice to come over the intercom.

"Branson, would you bring me and Miss Connelly two gigantic stacks of pancakes?" he asked, glancing into the master bathroom. "With the works. Syrup, whipped cream, a bunch of blueberries…"

The light was off in the bathroom, though, and nothing but silence met him. Her scent lingered on the bed, but he couldn't pick up any hints of it on the air. If she wasn't in the room, where was she?

"Have you seen Isabelle roaming around the house?"

"Sir, she left earlier this morning. Took a cab to the airport. She's taking the jet with the paintings back to Dublin."

"She—what?"

Terror tore through him like a knife.

"When I left your morning cup of coffee on the bedside table," he said, "I noticed a note from Miss Connelly. I left it where I found it."

Scrambling, Jack moved his cup and picked up the note. He read quickly, skimming, catching the highlights.

I'll send for you soon…you can meet me there in a few days…just need to make sure my father is all right… We'll figure this out, but I need a little time…I won't let you die, Jack, but I can't be here when my father's health is failing… he doesn't have long … If I woke you and said good-bye, I wouldn't have been strong enough to do what I have to do… please understand.

"Her poor father," he mumbled aloud, reading on. "She must be terrified."

He wanted nothing more than to hold her and ease her worry. At the last line, he stopped and read the words again.

I must be crazy, but I think I love you.

Happiness filled every corner of his soul, and he beamed. *She loves me.*

He'd done it. He wasn't going to waste away any longer. As quick as the elation danced through his veins, it was replaced with fear. She'd already left—gone back to Ireland. She couldn't leave now. He wouldn't let her go. Not when he was so close to having everything.

It couldn't have come at a better time, either. Blackouts were on the horizon, closing in fast, and after that... nothingness.

Desperation flooding in, Jack punched the intercom button. "How long ago did she leave, Branson?"

"Hours, sir." He paused. "The plane was loaded with her paintings and ready for takeoff, as you requested, so once she got on board, they departed."

She may've said she'd send for him soon, but he couldn't wait here with the taste of her flesh hanging on his lips and the memory of the way her body had felt beneath his. It'd be torture. Sheer agony.

"She left with the final painting," Branson added. "And might I add, it's a glorious painting. A real likeness."

Jack's brows pulled together in confusion. "Every Bella Nolan painting I own should already be on the plane. Which final piece are you talking about?"

"The one of you, sir," Branson said plainly. "*Werewolf in San Francisco.*"

"She took it?" Jaw clenching, he fought the urge to growl, burst through his skin, and shift into wolf form. "She said she was going to leave that one behind. I gave her every other one. Was it not enough?"

If he couldn't trust his fated mate, who *could* he trust?

She wanted to show her father the painting, and that's fine; he wouldn't have denied her if she'd asked. But *damn*. A dull aching pain spread through his middle and wormed its way into his chest.

He couldn't trust anyone anymore.

"I'm sorry, sir," Branson said. "I didn't know. I thought—"

"It's all right, Branson." He scrubbed his hand over his face as his stomach bottomed out. "You had no way to know."

Turning off the intercom, Jack swung his legs over the edge of the bed and sat up. His skin crawled. A wave of chills washed over him, and his stomach rumbled. Lifting his arms from his sides, Jack watched gooseflesh blanket them, followed by tremors.

"Oh, shit," he rasped out as the world zoomed in and out, in and out. "No, no, no—"

And then everything went black.

Chapter Fourteen

Neil picked Isabelle up from the Dublin airport, exactly as he said he would. Not that she'd ever doubted him. After stopping to refuel in JFK for an hour, Jack's jet landed at three thirty in the morning, Ireland time. To her, though, she'd traveled all day—missing it entirely—and it was nearly bedtime.

After securing transportation for her paintings from the airport to the museum, they drove an hour south, bypassing Dublin and Tallaght. On the drive to Glendalough, Neil traversed the narrow roads slickened with midnight rain and nagged her the whole way.

"You're crazy for even askin'," he said, weaving through the Wicklow Mountains. "You know your father won't want him here."

"I know, I know." She laid her head back against the headrest and let herself be mesmerized by the car's headlights sweeping over the empty road. "But you weren't there. You didn't meet him."

"Nor do I want to," Neil roared, taking the turns fast. "He belongs there, you belong here. It won't work, Isabelle. Get it out of your head now, before you talk to your dad."

It was going to be difficult to convince her father that Jack belonged in her life, but she had no idea Neil would be such a pain, too. Rather than fight an uphill battle on an empty stomach and a tired mind, she closed her eyes and pretended to sleep. Somewhere during her pretending, she actually dozed off, the rumbling of the car's engine dragging her into a deep sleep.

"Isabelle?"

Neil's voice. A hand on her shoulder, shaking.

"We're here," he said, louder. "Isabelle wake up."

Rubbing her hands over her eyes, she sat upright and took in the sights. Neil had parked in front of Connelly Castle so that it was in full view when she woke up. He was a great friend—one of the best. And he'd always watched out for her, knowing exactly what she needed. Even if she didn't.

Home.

Sixteen generations had been blessed to call Connelly Castle that, and she was proud to continue the line. The multi-bay Elizabethan-style castle stood majestically in the center of eight hundred acres of forest. Its stone-faced front, illuminated by bright white lights, seemed to welcome her home.

As she and Neil exited, grabbing her bags from the back, Isabelle rushed up the front stairs and pushed inside.

"He's upstairs," Neil said. "It's nearly five in the morn', so I'm sure he'll still be sleepin', but he probably wouldn't mind seeing you. He's been askin'."

Flushed with nerves, Isabelle ran up the red-carpeted stairs and turned down the narrow hall. She passed the first three doors, a medieval suit of armor, and then curved left, onto a staircase narrower than the first.

It was darker on the third floor, and the air couldn't circulate as well. Candles flickered from wrought iron sconces on the walls. Patterned rugs covered the floor, one on top of the next.

The decor in the castle hadn't changed in hundreds of years. Her father prided himself on keeping things the same. Traditional, no matter how restrictive.

Worry passed through her as she opened his door and let herself inside.

"Neil?" Her father coughed, jerking upright against the pillows on his headboard. "Is that you? Did you find my Belle?"

"It's me, Daddy." Running to his bedside, she knelt and took his hand. His skin was crackly and dry, and his cheeks had sunken in. Neil had been right—he didn't have long left. Days, maybe. "I'm here. I'm back."

He yawned. "Neil said you spent the weekend in San Francisco?"

"Did he?" Her voice squeaked. "What else did he say?"

"He said you attended a conference for Alpha heirs given by San Francisco's Alpha. He said Hayden Dean and his Luminary were going to talk about how to effortlessly take over the role of pack leader."

Of course that's what Neil told him.

It was exactly what he needed to hear.

"The conference wasn't all it was cracked up to be," she said slowly, drawing out the inevitable. "So I spent some time in the city, away from the conference hotel."

He twitched in bed and shifted his shoulders so that he faced her completely. "Didn't run into any trouble, did you?"

"Trouble?" She kissed the back of her daddy's hand and pressed it against her cheek. "No trouble. In fact—"

"Then you didn't run into anyone from the MacGrath family," he coughed out. His voice was a raspy whisper. Barely audible. "Bastards. Every one of 'em. Maybe the Alpha finally got wind of their conniving ways and pushed 'em out of the city."

No truce, then.

She'd been silly to hope that years gone by would've dulled the blade of retribution.

"Can I ask you something?" She shook with trepidation.

Coughing terribly, her father covered his mouth with the sleeve of his pajamas. "Anything, my dear."

Do you believe people can change? Have you met a MacGrath who wasn't as terrible as you thought he was? Are you able to forgive and forget?

"Do you think…"

As he rested his hand over his stomach, Isabelle caught sight of blood splatters staining the edge of his sleeve.

He was coughing up blood.

Her gaze held there as her stomach wrenched. Swallowing down the vile taste of fear and sorrow, she struggled to regain her composure and fight back her tears.

"Do you think…" She paused, uncertain how to proceed.

When put into perspective this way—on the very possible eve of his death—it didn't matter if her father could forgive and forget the MacGrath family. Only Jack. And there was no way she could talk about him now. Not like this.

She bowed her head to his hand. "I'd like to take you somewhere special tonight, just you and me. What do you think? Would you be up for it? Around eight?"

That would give her plenty of time to set everything up. She'd nap for a few hours, head to the gallery, and make sure the wolf pack's assistants had set up the display to her specifications. Highlighting *Werewolf in San Francisco* would lend the perfect opportunity to tell him about Jack and beg for his blessing.

"Of course." Her father cupped her chin in his hand, the way he used to when she was young, and said, "The doc was just saying I needed to move around today, get some fresh air. I haven't been out and about in weeks. It will be just what I need. Even if I didn't have the strength to move a muscle, nothing could stop me from going out with my girl. So... where are we headed?"

"It's a surprise."

"I don't normally like surprises," he went on, "but if it'll make you happy..."

There was more that'd make her happy than simply surprising him—being with Jack, for starters—but there'd be time to ease into that later.

. . .

When Jack regained consciousness, somewhere between "royally" and "fucked," he had the headache from hell and a bruise on his thigh. Branson had injected him with the recommended dose of adrenaline. Ten times over. He said if he'd administered any more, Jack might've gone into cardiac arrest.

It was a good thing the tenth one had worked, then.

By the time he came to and arranged for another private jet to take him to Dublin, it was just before nightfall. In Ireland, the moon was high in the sky, and Isabelle would probably be sleeping. She'd arrived somewhere in the early-morning hours of the day before, and would probably be exhausted from jetlag.

Too much time had passed.

He had to get to her.

Branson arranged everything. Transportation to and from the airport on both ends. He'd even made some calls and discovered the location of Connelly Castle, which was apparently the best-kept secret in all of Ireland. It was hidden deep in the Wicklow Mountains—the perfect place to hide from non-shifters, from what Branson's contact had said.

By the time Jack boarded the jet, his leg ached something fierce, and his skin had gone black at the injection point. His quadriceps looked raw and mangled, as if they'd been infected by some strange skin-eating bacteria.

The precise reason he hated using needles to get his high.

But if he was stuck on a plane for ten hours, what choice did he have? Not like he could jump out at 37,000 feet. And if he picked a fight with the steward or something—theoretically speaking, of course—they'd lock him up the moment they touched down in Dublin.

No, he didn't have a choice.

"Remember, the adrenaline shots may not work next time." Branson's voice rang in his ears. "I'll send you with a pack of twenty preloaded needles—super-high dosage in each one—but your body probably won't be able to handle the strain."

The warning had soured Jack's stomach, but he'd taken the backpack full of shots anyway, and kept them close to his seat as they lifted off and headed for Ireland.

Thankfully, he slept the whole flight. When he landed— two in the afternoon Ireland time—he made a beeline for the limousine waiting curbside at Dublin Airport. The sky was gloomy and gray as far as he could see in all directions. Rain fell to the ground in a constant and steady stream. No sign of breaking.

"Connelly Castle in the Wicklow Mountains," he ordered, clutching the backpack on his lap. "As fast as you can."

Although the driver looked at him strangely and insisted he'd never heard of Connelly Castle, he drove south of Dublin anyway, following the signs for the national forest. Some of the roads were insanely narrow—hardly earning the name of "road"—but the driver traversed them fearlessly. As if he'd grown accustomed to trucks speeding by in the opposite direction and nearly clipping his side-view mirror. More than once, Jack flinched from the closeness. The cars passed inches away, if that. Yet each brush with death, and every adrenaline rush, provided just the zing he needed.

Using the directions Branson had given him, Jack followed the route deep into the mountains, where paved roads gave way to gravel, and then to dirt. Sheep and cows peppered the countryside, grazing near rock walls and long-abandoned castle towers.

"I don't think you'll be findin' anything back here," the driver said, his Irish lilt lingering in Jack's ears. "You sure you want me to keep goin'?"

"Yes."

No hesitation. He hadn't come this far to give up and turn back now.

Rain battered the windows of the limo, and the driver clicked the windshield wipers on hyper-speed. They drove off-road for an additional twenty minutes, and finally turned into some sort of dirt driveway when the clock on the dash read three thirty.

Would he find Isabelle here? Would she be with her father or at the National Gallery of Ireland displaying *his* painting? Annoyance flared in him at her dismissal of her promise. She'd said she would take the other pieces and leave him that one. She knew how much that work meant to him. How could she rob him of the only thing that could heal the hurt caused by her absence?

"Well, I'll be jiggered," the driver swore, peering through the storm. "Look."

Up ahead, past a large, protective gate, a three-story stone mansion—no, a *castle*—came into view. It was situated in the middle of a grassy clearing with forest all around. Towers flanked the sides of the building—one tower had a glass-domed roof—and it looked as if some sort of garden courtyard stretched around the side and continued to the back.

"Thanks for the ride." Jack snatched the backpack carrying his necessities and stepped out into the rain.

He'd been close to his end for twenty years. Weakened and weary. Fighting off blackout spells. He'd stared death in the face and had been shaken to the bone.

But never, not once, had he ever been as afraid as he was in this moment.

Chapter Fifteen

Jack strode up to the gate as two guards—hundred-year-old werewolves from the smell of them—appeared from a shack on the right.

"Morning." The burlier of the two spoke first, his voice welcoming yet stern. He sniffed the air and grimaced. "You're far from your pack. Are you lost?"

"I'm looking for Isabelle Connelly, actually." He tightened the strap of the bag over his shoulder. "Is she here?"

"Is she expecting ya?" the shorter, squattier werewolf asked.

"Well, not exactly, but she'll be happy to see me." Jack tried smiling to loosen them up. "Trust me."

They stared, their faces remaining ugly, unreadable masks.

"Why don't you call her, then?" The burlier wolf shoved his hands in his pockets. "If you're friends, if she says it's all right for you to come in, we'll let you."

Fishing his phone out of his back pocket, Jack checked the screen and wagged it in the air. "No service."

"Out o' luck, then."

Jack approached the gate and grabbed the bars. "Listen, I

just want to talk to her for a few minutes, and I'm not leaving until I do."

And while he was there, he'd talk to her father, too. They could have a conversation like two civilized businessmen. Jack would politely ask for his daughter's hand and prove, once and for all, that what happened in the past should stay there. He was not his parents or grandparents. He did not lie, cheat, and steal to get ahead. He'd made his living honorably.

He'd spend every day of his life making her happiness his number one priority. And if her happiness depended on taking care of pack business, he'd support her in that, too. He'd even consider moving to Ireland. The land was lush and rich, steeped in culture and legend. And the people were rumored to be friendly and welcoming…not that he could say with the pissed-off guards standing in front of him, blocking his way.

"I don't think he's gettin' it," the hulky one said to his friend.

"You're right. He's not." The shorter one disappeared to the shack and came back holding a black club with a ball on the end that zinged with electricity. "He'll get the message one way or another."

Banging the club along the bars, they came to life, charged with volts of electricity. With a curse, Jack removed his hands and rubbed them on his pants to wipe off the lingering shock.

"Isabelle!" Cupping his hands over his mouth, Jack bellowed toward the castle. His hands shook. Just one hard quake that reverberated up his arm. *Shit.* "Isabelle, can you hear me?"

"You can scream until you're blue. You're not going in, and she's not comin' out."

A loud bleeping sound came from the guard shack. Eyeing him skeptically, Hulk marched to the right and out of sight.

"Yes, sir," he said. "There's a werewolf here who says he's looking for Isabelle." Long, deadening pause. "I'm not sure, let me check. Hey, American."

Jack stared.

Squatty hit the bars with his staff. "He means you."

"Yeah?"

"Where you from?"

As his hands began to tremble, harder now, Jack folded his arms over his chest. If someone was asking where he was from, it definitely wasn't Isabelle calling the guard shack to let him in.

"San Francisco," he answered hesitantly.

The pack didn't take well to foreigners, especially someone bearing the MacGrath name.

After relaying the message, Hulk then hung up the phone. With a sharp buzz, the gate lock clicked and the doors swung open. Hope speared through him. She was there after all. But then why—

"Someone wants to talk to you." Hulk grabbed him by the elbow as Squatty ripped his backpack away from him.

"Hey, hey, wait a second." Jack reached for his bag, but was jerked away down the path toward the castle.

At least he was moving in the right direction.

"Precautionary search," Squatty snapped, digging through his things. "Change of clothes, toothbrush, pack of...*medical supplies*? What's with all the needles?"

"I'm diabetic." Jack spouted the first thing that came to mind. "It's my insulin. I need that."

Holding the backpack tight, the guards trudged up the steps, dragging Jack along. Pushing through the massive wooden front doors, Isabelle's scent struck him. He growled deep in his chest at the aroma, and then was stunned silent. The interior of the castle was even more impressive than the exterior. Ancient tapestries hung from the stone walls. Ornate red and gold rugs covered the floor. Candles flickered everywhere: sconces, five-tier wrought iron chandeliers, on every single stair winding to the left of the entry. Medieval suits of armor stood gallant watch from the balcony and insets in the walls.

This was Isabelle's home?

No wonder she held so tightly to tradition. One step into her family's castle and he'd teleported back to the early 1800s. Nothing had changed.

And if he didn't get to talk to her father, nothing ever would.

Jerked into a study on the right, Hulk tossed Jack onto a blue velvet couch and closed the heavy doors behind them.

"Where's Isabelle?" he asked, catching his backpack when Squatty tossed it at him. "Is she coming down?"

"You're going to wait here," Hulk grumbled.

Each guard stood in front of an entrance, watching Jack. Waiting for him to move. When a second door into the study opened to Jack's left, he jumped to his feet.

"Isabelle?"

A dark-haired werewolf with angry blue eyes walked in, leveling Jack with a glare meant to scare him out of Ireland. But he wasn't going anywhere without his Luminary. He remained standing.

"Where is she?" he asked.

"I'm Neil. A longtime friend of Isabelle's."

A streak of possession rumbled through him like thunder. "Then you know where I can find her."

Neil moved around Jack, studying him, giving away nothing. "You're going to talk to me first, before anything happens, and you're going to answer my questions whether you like them or not. When did you get in?"

What choice did Jack have other than to talk? He didn't want to fight Isabelle's friends and family to get to her—talk about making a wrong first impression—but how else could he find her?

"About two hours ago," he answered flatly. "Listen, Neil,

I'm not going to harm Isabelle or anyone here. I'm not a threat of any kind. If you could—"

"Oh, but you are a threat, Mr. MacGrath."

He knows my name.

"You're dumber than you look if you think we're just going to let you walk in here and try to take Isabelle away from us."

Jack raised his chin. "What if she wants to leave with me?"

"She doesn't know what she wants." Neil paced around Jack in a tight circle, sizing him up, bumping into his shoulder with every turn. "It's a very hard time in her life right now , and she got caught up in something she wasn't prepared for. All you're going to do by being here is stir trouble where it doesn't need stirrin'."

"I need to see her." He turned to face him. "You're not going to stop me."

Neil's light eyes widened with awareness. He must've picked up on the aggression surging through Jack's veins.

"For the last two hundred years, my job has been to care for the Connelly family," he said. "To protect them at all costs. Before you stepped into the picture, Isabelle was focused and determined. She was happy. With you, there's only a future filled with shame and heartbreak."

"You don't know that," Jack bit out, staring him down. "You don't know how we are together and what kind of a future we could have."

"I know there are traditions we hold dear, and customs you know nothing about. How can you expect to step into something when you're an outsider?"

"Enlighten me, then."

Neil's nostrils flared. "The Alpha must give his blessing for the heir to marry and bond with another. Her whole life, Isabelle has dreamed of making her father, and the pack, proud. She craves his blessing and his approval more than anyone else's. And there's no way he'd ever give his blessing to you. A MacGrath." He scoffed, the corners of his lips twisting up. "You were stupid to come here. It's time for you to go."

And then Neil grabbed for Jack's arm

"Don't touch me." Jack twisted out of his hold. "I'm not going anywhere until I see her for two seconds. I need to know she's all right."

"Of course she's all right." Neil latched onto Jack's arm again. "This is her home. She's with family now, the people who truly love her."

Good jab, bastard.

Realization trickled into his chest. Neil wasn't going to let Jack see her. This whole meet-up was a way to check him out, evaluate his intent, and then kick him out on his ass.

Better make his resolve crystal clear, then.

"I'm her family now," Jack said, grinding his back teeth together. "No one is going to change that. Not you, and certainly not Tweedle-Dee and Tweedle-Dum over there."

With a growl, Jack rushed Neil, slamming him into a large suit of armor standing against the side entrance. As they tangled, arms grappling, Jack sensed the guards coming to Neil's aid.

It was about to be three against one.

And he was on their turf.

Surges of aggression thrummed through his veins, boiling and churning in his gut. His vision blurred. Hands shook. Legs wobbled. And then they overtook him, tackling him to the ground.

But it was too late.

Energy whipped through him like a snake. Huddled on the ground, he clenched, head to toe. Balled the shifting sensations in his middle, and then pushed outward, releasing his full fury. Blasting into wolf form in a flurry of fur and shredded clothes, he tossed the guards aside. Barreled through the study doors and into the foyer. Thinking fast, he darted up the stairs.

Isabelle.

I have to get to her.

Behind him, footsteps followed, stomping up the stairs. They were closing in, shouting. Barking orders.

Picking up Isabelle's scent, Jack curved right at the top of the stairs, his back legs hitting the banister as he cut the turn short. Charging down the hall, fueled by anger and hatred, love and determination, her scent hit him.

Left turn.

Banking hard, he leaped up another set of stairs and squished his burly body up a narrower corridor than the first.

More shouts from behind him. They were desperate now.

He must be close to finding her.

Reaching the top of the second set of stairs, he rushed the closed door. Her scent was stronger here—she'd either been here recently, or was still inside.

Isabelle.

Bursting through, shattering the wood to splinters, Jack charged inside and used his heightened senses to search through the dark.

He skidded to a stop. Padded forward, toward a gigantic four-poster bed, and a worn and weathered werewolf sitting up against the headboard. The smell of death permeated Jack's senses, burning his nose.

"I'm Gerard Connelly," the man said, sitting upright. "Who the *hell* are you, and what are you doing breaking into my home?"

Shit.

Not the introduction he would've liked to have with his future father-in-law.

Jack gulped, panting, searching the dark corners of the room for his love. And was tackled from behind by three infuriated Irish wolves.

Chapter Sixteen

As Jack shifted back to human form, Hulk and Squatty looped their arms through his and jerked him to his feet.

"Hold him still so I can get a good look at him," Gerard commanded.

Neil stood behind Jack, his thick hands around his neck, ready to snap it at a moment's notice. He squirmed to be free, but the guards were huge. Stronger and more relentless than they appeared. And he'd spent too much of his waning strength during the shift.

"I'm sorry, sir," Neil said from behind Jack. "We had him in the study, but he took us off guard, shifted, and—"

Gerard put up a hand, silencing him, and then set his gaze on Jack. "Who are you? A thief?"

"I'm not a thief." Jack shook his head, painfully aware how stark naked he was. "I came here to talk to your daughter."

Eyes widening, Gerard snapped toward Neil. "Get this man some clothes. I will not continue to talk to him this way."

They waited in silence, measuring each other up, until Neil brought the T-shirt and jeans Jack had packed in his bag. He chucked them at Jack's middle. Releasing his arms, Hulk and Squatty stood by while Jack dressed...and then they snatched him up again. *Idiots.* If he'd really wanted to attack Gerard, he would've done it in those few precious seconds when he was naked and unrestrained.

"That's better," Gerard said, his mouth a hard line.

"Isabelle..." Jack started.

"We're lucky she's not here." Gerard's gaze eyes burned with wicked amusement. "You might've gotten to her before we could get our hands on you. And I believe I asked you who you were."

She wasn't here?

Despair hollowed him out. "My name is Jack MacGrath."

"MacGrath?" The word was a growl, spoken short and clipped. Gerard fumed, his jaw clenching and unclenching. "Then you are a thief. And you're also a liar and a conspirator, and bear one of the vilest names on the planet. What are you doing in my home?"

"I'm here for Isabelle."

Gerard paused, measuring him with beady onyx eyes. With a quick flip of the covers, he swung his legs over the side of the bed and stood on shaky legs. He was tall. Six foot five, maybe? But his skin was pasty and his eyes sunken in. Even in his weakened state, her father stood tall, his shoulders pulled back. Shuffling over to Jack, he glowered, looking as if he planned to rip Jack's head off his neck.

"How do you know my daughter?" he growled, coming closer.

The guards tightened their grip on Jack, as if he'd try to attack their Alpha. But he'd told them before—he wasn't here to hurt anyone.

"Isabelle came to San Francisco over the weekend, and we met—"

"Were you in the Alpha's heir conference, too?" He

grimaced as if he'd tasted something sour. "I can't imagine you being Alpha of anything."

Alpha heir conference?

"No, sir, I'm not going to be Alpha. I met her at an art auction on Saturday morning."

Neil dug his fingers into Jack's neck and squeezed tight. Air wheezed in and out of his lungs until words vanished and he couldn't go on. He hadn't forgotten what Isabelle had told him. She'd wanted to surprise her father with the collection. Jack wasn't going to spoil that, as Neil obviously thought. But he also wasn't going to lie to her father about where and how they met, either.

He'd already started off on the wrong foot, barging into his private chamber. He wasn't going to add lying to the mix.

"She said nothing of an art auction." Gerard frowned. "And she said nothing of you."

That burned, even though it was expected.

"Isabelle and I..." He'd walked through his moment in his mind, had gone over and over how he was going to say this to her father. But now that he stared into his sunken face, the words disappeared. "...I want to be with her."

I need to be with her. She's my Luminary. My soul howls for her.

That's what he'd wanted to say.

"You want to court my Isabelle?" Gerard stalked closer, within arm's reach. And then he laughed. The guards chuckled and then broke into laughter with him. "There's a chance you're even dumber than your ancestors." He belted out a laugh that echoed into the room. "I didn't think that was possible, but here you stand."

Oh, there'd be no softening her father for the blow. No way to ease him into the idea that they belonged together. He saw that now, and understood Isabelle's predicament.

But he had a dilemma, too. If they didn't bond soon, he

wouldn't live to see the coming year.

"The fights and lies between our families happened hundreds of years ago," Jack said. "That's got nothing to do with me and your daughter. Right here, as I stand before you this day, I can say with every beat of my heart that I'm in love with her, and she's in love with me. And that's the way it will be until the end of time."

Gerard's laugh cut short. Blistering waves of rage radiated from his body. As he narrowed his eyes to slits, Gerard coldcocked him. Right in the nose. Starbursts went off behind his eyes. Blood gushed from his nose, dripping down his chest to the floor.

For a guy on his deathbed, he could deliver one hell of a blow.

"How dare you," Gerard seethed. "You claim to be different from your ancestors, yet what have you done? You've barged into my home uninvited and unannounced, terrorized my guards, and while in San Francisco, you attempted to steal the one thing that means the most to me in this world. You are exactly as I thought you were—exactly like every other MacGrath I've ever met. You are a liar, a thief, a greedy bastard."

Well, when he put it like that…

"It would seem that way, but—"

"But nothing." Gerard's expression went bitter. "You could never be good enough for Isabelle."

At least they agreed on that point. She was an angel. He didn't deserve her, but would spend the rest of his life striving to be the man she needed.

"She loves me."

Gerard squinted, his nostrils flaring. "Has she told you so?"

The words she'd scribbled came to him: *I must be crazy, but I think I love you.*

She hadn't said it, exactly. She *thought* she loved him.

Sensing Jack's hesitation, Gerard grinned from the side of his mouth. "She hasn't said a thing…you don't even know how she feels." He paused, searching Jack's face, and then, "Let me tell you what I know. The MacGrath family is filled with selfish creatures who are only out for their own gain. They'll do anything to get what they want. When given the chance, you'll put your own happiness first. You'll prioritize your needs above hers. Every single time. It's ingrained in you to be that way. You can't help it. But I can stop it from happening in the first place." He nudged his chin at each of the guards. "Take him to the dungeon."

"What?" Desperate, Jack fought to get free, but they held impossibly tight. Horror pierced him. "No, wait. The *dungeon*?"

"You'll like it down there," Gerard said, turning back to his bed. "It's full of your kind."

"My kind?"

Americans? Perceived liars or criminals?

Glancing over his shoulder, Gerard grinned sadistically. "Rats."

There was the adrenaline he'd been missing. Swells of the energizing hormone flooded his veins at the thought of rats crawling over his body. His eyes went wide as sparks flared in his chest.

Leaving Neil in the chamber with Gerard, the two guards dragged Jack out of the room. Kicking and hollering, Jack struggled. Clashed against the guard on either arm. He tried to shift, summoning the energy surging through him. But the transformation didn't come.

He'd expended too much energy earlier, and the quick spark he'd gotten from the mention of the rats hadn't been enough to recharge him.

Spiraling down the first and second staircases, they

manhandled him as if they'd done this before. As they passed the study, he caught sight of his backpack on the floor near the couch where he'd been sitting.

Damn it.

"Hey, hey, wait." He skidded his feet. Pulled and tugged to move toward the study. "My bag, my insulin. Can you grab it and bring it down into the cell—er, dungeon—with me? We're civilized men, enemies or not."

They didn't flinch, didn't respond.

The blood drained from his veins. "It's my life we're talking about."

"Exactly, MacGrath." Hulk laughed, low and husky. "It's your life."

Dragging him away from the study, they turned right and passed through a door hidden beneath the stairs. Walls made of stone lined a narrow spiral staircase that descended into the dark. Fighting the whole way, Hulk and Squatty eventually managed to get Jack to the bottom. They spilled out into some sort of dimly lit cave with small tunnels branching off in every direction. It was colder down here, the air stagnant and chilling. The walls were smooth and glistening. Like damp limestone. Water trickled somewhere in the distance, and the pungent stench of ancient grime permeated Jack's senses.

"Where do all those tunnels lead?" Jack searched around, scoping out a route to use when they finally left him to his own devices. "To the seventh circle of hell?"

"It's an escape route," Hulk said, cinching Jack's hands behind his back. "Some of these tunnels go on for miles and dead end. Others loop around to other tunnels. And one spits out somewhere on the River Avonmore."

"One?" Jack blanched, staring at the nine tunnels branching off. "And all these others lead nowhere?"

"Well, yeah," Squatty said. "During an escape, the Connellys would know which tunnel led out, but the attackers wouldn't. They'd get a clean break."

It was quite brilliant, actually.

But he had to get out, and didn't have time to search around. There was nothing for him down here. No way to get the thrills he needed to survive. He'd be dead in days without it. But Isabelle would have to come back to the castle for her father. Would he hear her when she did? Would she detect his scent, know he'd come, and search him out?

God, he hoped so.

And before it was too late.

"This way," Hulk grumbled, and led Jack to the far wall, where giant steel hooks had been drilled into the stone. Chains looped through the hooks and hung to the floor with heavy shackles attached to the end.

"You're kidding," Jack said, going cold. "This isn't the Middle Ages, you know. Prisons have advanced since then. Three square meals a day, a bed, and wifi. This is—"

"The way we do it here," Squatty interrupted, slamming Jack against the wall. He locked Jack's wrists into the top shackles as Hulk attached his ankles to the bottom ones. "You'll only be down here until our Alpha decides exactly what to do with you."

Still, he dared not hope.

After checking the shackles, Squatty and Hulk strode toward the stairs leading to the main floor of the castle. As if to follow them, Jack pulled away from the wall, the shackles oppressively heavy on his hands and feet. The chains gave him about five feet of walking room, but the hooks were pinned solidly into the stone.

They left him in the dark with no adrenaline to stay alive, and only a grim sliver of hope in his heart. As if his body knew when things had become dire, his hands started to tremble, vibrating through his arms, and chest.

"Oh yeah," he mumbled, steeling himself for the

inevitable. "This is the perfect time to black out."

And then high-pitched squeaking sounds echoed through the tunnels.

Rats.

Chapter Seventeen

As the clock clicked ten past eight, Isabelle searched around Bella Nolan's area of the National Gallery of Ireland one more time. Each piece of art had been hung and illuminated. They were all there, including the one she'd painted of Neil at the Cliffs of Moher for his mother.

And they were perfect.

In the center of the room, she'd highlighted *Werewolf in San Francisco,* her favorite piece. Heart pinching, she swept her fingers over the wolf in the painting, over Jack's coat. She'd painted him perfectly, capturing the gleam in his eye and the strength in his stance. Skin chilling, she brushed her hands over her arms and recalled how that night had ended.

There was so much riding on tonight and her father's reaction.

While she thought of it, *where was he?*

Anticipation pulsed through her as she exited the museum and waited at the bottom of the steps for her father's car to appear. Neil had said he'd bring him by eight sharp. It was ten past.

Her father was never late.

Something must've held him up. She would've been worried it was his health, but Neil would've called. What, then?

As she checked her phone to see if she'd missed a message, a blacked-out Lincoln pulled up. Her dad's car. *He was here.* Neil exited first and swept around the back.

"We have a problem." Popping the trunk, he pulled out a wheelchair and readied it for her father. "He's not in the best mood."

Oh, great.

"What happened?"

The back door opened and her father stepped out. "Nothing I want to worry you with at the moment."

Standing back with his arms folded over his chest, Neil pressed his lips into a tight line. There was something he wanted to add…

"We can talk about it later." Her father eased into the wheelchair. "For now, I want to spend a wonderful night with my daughter, and think about nothing else. It's exactly the thing that will cheer me up. Now what is this surprise you have for me?"

Whatever had stalled him, it must not have been too important. Although Neil looked stressed, her father appeared fine. Sure, he was weak, but he was still interested in what she had planned, which was a bonus.

"Right this way, Dad." She took the handles from Neil, though he held tight.

"We have to talk," Neil gritted through clenched teeth.

Impatient to show her father, when they were so close, she glared. "We can talk after, okay? Circle the block, see a show, run errands, I don't care. Pick him up in two hours."

"If you insist." With a small, respectful head nod, Neil marched toward the driver's side door. "I suppose the *problem* isn't going anywhere."

What had he meant by that?

"Take me away, Isabelle," her father said.

"Sure thing." She pushed him toward the museum entrance, and then leaned close to his ear. "I know you're not an art fan, but I heard there's an exhibit in one of the halls that will take your breath away."

"You think so?"

He sounded disbelieving.

And it hurt.

"I do," she said, and rolled him inside. "It's taken me a long time to put this together, so I really hope you can appreciate it."

"Wait." He twisted in his chair. Craned to look over his shoulder. "You put together the exhibit?"

She didn't answer as she whisked him toward the Bella Nolan area. He'd see the truth with his own eyes.

"Does this have to do with the art auction you went to in the States?"

She paused, hesitating. Thinking back. Had she mentioned it when she was at his bedside? No, she hadn't. Must've been Neil.

"Yes," she said finally. "It does, but there's so much more to it than that."

Slowing around the final corner, dizziness swept over her and her skin prickled with gooseflesh. She was nervous beyond belief. Her father wouldn't physically destroy all of the paintings as he'd done with the first one, but his disapproval could devastate her just the same.

"Okay," she said more to herself than to him. "Here it is. A collection of art by the internationally renowned artist Bella Nolan."

As she pushed him into the center of the gallery, she could sense his heartbeat slow. His breathing matched. He leaned forward in his chair. But she couldn't pick up any emotions from him. Not anger or cynicism, happiness or surprise. Nothing.

Anxiety spiraled within her as she rolled him toward *Werewolf at the Cliffs of Moher.* "The entire collection is called *Urban Werewolves,* though not all of them were painted that way. Look, this one is of Neil."

"Our Neil?" he leaned forward, eyeing the art curiously. "I never knew he volunteered for art sessions. Look at that."

Had he made the connection? He didn't seem to have. The worry in her veins eased away as she pushed him along, mentioning small tidbits about each of the paintings.

"This one was where you and mom went on your honeymoon, remember?"

That one got a smile out of him. "Of course I remember. That wolf is strong, isn't he? Look at him. How vibrant and full of life."

"And this one—" She moved him toward *Werewolf in Manhattan.* "Remember when you and mom took me to New York? The skyline was amazing."

He nodded. "That was a great trip."

Why wasn't he saying anything else? Did he not see the resemblance between the painting she'd done of him in wolf form in front of Saint Patrick's Cathedral and these? Had her first painting meant so little to him that he didn't even remember it?

Heart in her throat, she escorted him to Jack's painting. "This one is called *Werewolf in San Francisco.*"

"It's striking."

"I'm so glad you think so." Joy lit her up. Locking the wheels of his chair, she came around and knelt beside him. "Father, now I'd like to introduce you to Bella Nolan."

He stuck out his hand. "Nice to meet you, sweetheart."

"You…" Thoughts whirling, tears seized her throat. Her

heart hiccuped and then began hammering against her ribs. She couldn't find the words. Wrapping her arms around his neck, she squeezed him tight. "You *do* remember."

He'd made the connection. Maybe the first painting really had made an impression on him. She sucked in a rattled breath as her heartbeat echoed in her ears.

"Of course I remember." He pulled back and stroked his hands down her hair. "Isabelle, I could never forget. I simply thought painting was a distraction for you, something that would turn your focus away from ruling the pack someday. There's a lot to learn about pack dynamics and foreign policy, my dear, and you have to give it the attention that it deserves."

"I know that." Heart racing, she kneeled beside his chair. "I do."

"To be honest, I thought this was a hobby—a onetime thing. I didn't realize"—his gaze skimmed the gallery, stopping on every single piece in turn—"it would turn into something like this. It's astonishing. Truly."

It was everything she'd always dreamed of hearing.

As she blinked, and swallowed down the sting in her throat, a single tear rolled down her cheek. "It's not a hobby… it never was. It's my passion, Father. Something that makes me happy. I'm not going to turn away from ruling the pack, but I want to do this, too."

Now came the words ripped straight from her heart…

"I wanted you to understand how important this is to me before you…" The words were strangled out of her, along with all the air in her lungs.

He nodded, placing his hand over hers as it rested on the arm of his wheelchair. "Before I died," he finished for her. "It's okay, Isabelle."

"I've kept this a secret far too long."

"Judging from how many paintings there are," he said, spreading his arms wide, "you've done a mighty good job keeping it. Have they been on display here this whole time?"

"No," she said, grinning proudly. "They were sold all over the world, some of them for hundreds of thousands of dollars."

"Really?" He snapped his gaze to hers. "Are you telling me I have a famous daughter?"

As a warm blush crept into her cheeks, she shook her head humbly. "No, but some of them are worth more than you'd believe."

The one directly in front of them was priceless…

"How did you get them all here?" He touched the bottom of Jack's painting. "Did you have to buy them back?"

"Some yes, but others are more complicated to explain." Her heart beat fast. "Father, painting has become a part of me, as much as breathing, eating, and loving. I want to keep doing it, for as long as I can, but I desperately need your blessing."

"Oh sweetheart, you have it." He spread his arms wide, and she nearly leaped into them. "All I ever wanted was for you to be happy with the life I've made for you. I didn't realize this meant so much to you, but seeing them all lined up this way…" He paused as if he was choking up. "If you've found your happiness painting, I don't see any reason why you'd have to choose between them now."

Her heart soared, releasing the weight she'd been bearing for so long.

"Thank you so much," she cried. "You have no idea what that your blessing means to me, how important is that I know you want me to be happy, no matter what."

"Always," he said, brushing a hand down her cheek. "Whatever it takes, you should follow your heart."

"God, I'm so glad to hear you say that." She moved closer to Jack's painting. "Because I have fallen in love with painting…and with someone I'm not sure you'll approve of."

Her dad's smile faltered.

"This is him," she said, pointing to the wolf in the painting.

"I met him in San Francisco and painted him in Golden Gate Park. He let me borrow a lot of these from his private gallery because he knew how much it'd mean to me to display them for you."

Folding his arms over his chest, her father got the strangest look on his face. As if he were contemplating something that had him torn to pieces. His brows knit together, his dark eyes shadowed over, and his lips pulled down into a frown.

"What's his name?" he asked.

"Jack"—she swallowed hard—"MacGrath."

She winced, waiting for him to lose his cool. Scream and yell and tell her how foolish she was to start something with him.

"*A stor*, Isabelle….my treasure." He motioned for her to come back down to his side. As she did, he took her hand. "I love you. More than anything. More than life itself. There is nothing I wouldn't do to see you happy in this life. And that's the reason I can't let you be with him."

She frowned. Not the reaction she'd been expecting. His response seemed practiced. It was lacking anger, and instead, seemed rehearsed with a calm clarity that only time could offer.

"I don't understand," she said. "If you want me to be happy, why can't I be with someone who makes me that way? He's not anything like the other MacGrath family members you've told me about. He's kind and gentle, and wants me to be happy, just as you do."

He scoffed. "Isabelle, MacGrath men never put another's happiness over their own. Not ever. If Jack MacGrath gave you his paintings to bring here, he must be getting something out of the deal."

What could he possibly be gaining by letting her borrow his collection? If anything, she'd taken from him. Especially since she took the one painting he loved most. Without asking.

If anyone was the thief, it was her, really.

"All you have to do is figure out what your precious Jack wants most," her father said. "And then ask yourself, can he get that from you? If the answer's yes, you know he's like every other MacGrath in his family line. Only with you, stringing you along, so that he can get what he wants."

From nearly the moment she met Jack, he'd made it perfectly clear that he wanted her and no other. More than that, he wanted to bond with her.

So that he could live.

As the thought struck her, her father squeezed her hand.

"I hate that I'm right all the time," he said, "but I'm an excellent judge of character. Show me a MacGrath who'd put someone else's needs above his own, and I might change my tune. Until then, you have my blessing to paint and travel and rule the pack after me. But you do not have my blessing to be with Jack MacGrath."

He'll die without me.

She was going to be sick. Head spinning, stomach souring, Isabelle hung her head in her hands. Every muscle in her body tightened to the point of pain, and her heart—good God, her heart—clenched into a rock.

She'd gotten what she'd always wanted: her father's blessing to paint.

But she'd have to continue on with life, missing one half of her heart.

Chapter Eighteen

Jack searched through the dark, kicking rats as they came close. The mangy varmints were really emerging from the tunnels now. They must've smelled desperation, and it was seeping from his pores.

He'd been down here for an hour. Maybe two? He'd managed to ward off the fainting spells as they washed over him—might've had something to do with the possibility that rats would gnaw on his lifeless body while he was out. He was more determined than ever to stay alert and stay awake until Isabelle came back.

A door slammed on the floor above him. Heavy footsteps pounded down the stairs. Readying for a fight, Jack did a quick flip of the chains on his wrists, so that he was holding down about a foot on each side.

All he'd have to do is get close enough to throw the slackened chains around Hulk's or Squatty's neck. He'd cross his arms as he threw, creating a loop—a noose, in this case—and bear down.

It was his only chance for escape.

Pretending to be tired and weak—something he knew how to pretend damn well—he backed against the stone. Slouched against the wall, and dropped his head lifelessly to his shoulder.

Squatty appeared at the base of the stairs carrying a sandwich and a bottle of water. "Rise and shine, MacGrath," he said. "I brought dinner."

Jack didn't move. Not a muscle.

"Hey, MacGrath." Squatty stalked closer. "You hear what I said? I've got dinner. If you don't want it, I'll feed it to the rats."

Please don't let him toss it from there.

He needed to come closer.

Playing the part, Jack opened his mouth as if he wanted to say something. But he whispered the words, as hoarse as he could. And then with a limp wrist, he clutched at his throat.

"Somethin' wrong, MacGrath?" Squatty knelt out of reach of the chains. "Speak up."

Jack pretended to try again, amping up the dramatics. He raised his left hand to his throat, crossing it over the right, and this time he made his hands shake.

"Help," he rasped. Coughed. Faked a choke. "Can't… breathe."

"What the hell happened to ya?"

Squatty came close, within reach if Jack got up and charged. But he only had one shot at this, and he needed to be closer.

"Rats," Jack mumbled.

It was all he could think to say, even though it didn't make any damn sense.

"Rats?" Squatty's eyes went wide in shock as he knelt close, getting comfortable with Jack's weakened state. *Sucker.* "One jump down your throat or somethin'?"

This guy wasn't bright, but he was perfect.

Using every last ounce of energy he had, Jack threw his arms into the air toward Squatty. Crossed his wrists. Let the slack on the chains loose. Squatty reacted, but it was too late. The chains circled around his neck. With his arms crossed, Jack slid back onto the floor and yanked hard, bringing Squatty crashing on top of him. And then, when Squatty was gasping and spitting for air, clawing at the chains around his neck, Jack rolled. Flipped him onto his back. Knelt over him, a knee to his chest, the chains tight around his neck.

Squatty punched and kicked to get free, but Jack dodged the blows. He took a few knees to the back, but within a few seconds, the lack of air must've gotten to Squatty. Eyes rolling back, his mouth fell open. His head fell, hitting the stone with a dull *thud*.

After making sure he really was passed out, Jack released him.

Didn't want to kill the sucker, after all.

But he did need the key to the shackles. And the sandwich.

After finding the key to the cuffs in Squatty's back pocket, Jack freed himself. Shoving the sandwich in his mouth, Jack dragged Squatty up the stairs and onto the main floor where the rats wouldn't get him. Since the guards were in the castle, he'd planned to go out one of the tunnels, but now, as he pushed out the door beneath the stairs, not a single questionable scent hit him.

Where was everyone?

Tiptoeing out, Jack's bare feet slid over the hardwood. He wouldn't make it far without shoes. Scanning the study for this boots and his backpack with the adrenaline shots, he came up empty.

"They took the damn bag." His stomach fell. "What the hell am I going to do?"

Voices from upstairs.

"Shit."

Scurrying back to the hall, Jack ripped the boots from Squatty's feet and shoved them on his own. The boots were a tight fit, but they would do the trick. He needed shoes to run faster.

That was all that mattered.

More voices. Hulk's scent. He was coming.

Pushing out the front doors and into the night, Jack made a beeline around the house and searched for a garage.

There. Three bays. Looked like a workshop of sorts.

Sprinting along the side, a door came into view. *Unlocked.* He slipped inside, shutting it behind him, and searched the dark. The garage could've easily fit two cars, but the stalls were empty.

Gerard had said Isabelle wasn't home. Her father meant the world to her. If she wasn't with him in his weakened state, he instinctively knew where she'd be.

Readying the paintings in Dublin.

The garage stalls may've been empty, but against the far wall a tarp had been draped over something bulky. Striding over, unease settling in his gut, he yanked off the cover.

A black Bandit motorcycle. Looked to be a few years old, but someone had taken the time to clean it. And had been dumb enough to leave the key in the ignition.

Please start.

Walking the bike out so as not to alert Hulk or anyone else in the castle, Jack punched the button in the guard shack to open the gate—the same one he'd watched Hulk push to let him in. Once out of the gate, he straddled the bike, brought the engine roaring to life, and took off north, following signs to Dublin.

The ride was cold and wet, as a fierce rainstorm moved over the Wicklow Mountains, following his route. His T-shirt and jeans were drenched, and his skin was covered with chills. By the time he reached the outskirts of the city, he was trembling head to foot.

Was it from the weather? Pre-blackout?

He couldn't tell, but had come too far to let anything stop him now.

He had to see Isabelle. Once she saw the state he was in—the state her father had put him in—she'd run to him. Choose him over her father. They'd bond. And he wouldn't have to worry about blacking out ever again.

So close.

He sped past Saint Patrick's Cathedral, City Hall, and Trinity College, catching every green light on the way. He'd never blown through so many intersections in his life. It was as if fate wanted him to have a clear shot while he raced to his Luminary's side. Still, drivers honked. Pedestrians hollered, giving him a fist in the air as he waved apologetically. A few close calls and adrenaline bursts later, the National Gallery of Ireland appeared on the right. He pulled up to the front, dismounted the bike, and darted up the steps.

Isabelle's unmistakable scent struck him the moment he stepped inside. Mixed with it was the pungent stench of death.

Her father was here.

Following the pull in his gut, Jack trudged over the glistening floors, leaving a trail of rainwater behind. It spilled from his body and clothes and squeaked in the soles of his mis-sized shoes.

"Where are you?" he mumbled to himself, shuffling through the museum. "I have to see you."

One look at Isabelle's angelic face and he'd feel better. He'd fill with warmth and light, and then, once her father saw them together, he wouldn't be able to deny their connection. He'd see Isabelle's face light up. He'd know, once and for all, that Jack was the one who could make her happy.

He'd have to give his blessing then.

As he turned through a massive archway, *Werewolf in*

Venice came into view. And then *Werewolf in Manhattan*. And *Werewolf in Moscow.*

He froze. Taking in the way each of her paintings had been displayed.

The spread was magnificent. Everything she'd dreamed it would be. Her work was breathtaking in his private gallery, but it was safe there. No threat of non-shifters seeing it. When displayed out in the open this way, with werewolves revealed on canvas, there was a sense of vulnerability coupled with it. The whole thing made him feel somehow light and free.

"You did it," he whispered.

And then he saw her.

Isabelle stood with her back to him, facing her father and *Werewolf in San Francisco.* Although she was standing in front of her father, blocking his face, his arms were folded over his chest, and his foot tapped angrily against the foothold of his wheelchair.

He wasn't happy.

She'd told him.

Straining, Jack used his heightened hearing to listen for the inflections in her voice.

"I know you said you'd never give your blessing," she pleaded. Her voice cracked—a blow to his heart. "But isn't there anything he could do to win your favor?"

Desperate to hear, Jack darted behind a stone pillar separating one gallery from another. He'd do anything to have her. And if her father had any conditions for them to be together, it was done.

"He could be born to different parents." Gerard took her hand and set it on his lap. "He could have been raised as part of the Irish wolf pack. Short of those things, it's not going to happen. Isabelle, he's not one of us. He's simply not."

"But I love him, Father. I do."

She loves me.

Everything in Jack's body screamed to run to her, haul her into his arms, and take her away from here. But he waited, listening, heart leaping out of his chest.

"Do you love me?" her father asked.

She shifted the weight on her feet back and forth. "You know I do."

"And do you love the pack?"

"As my brothers and sisters," she said, nodding.

"Then you must not turn your back on them, on me. Your responsibility lies with the pack. It always has. You were born with the task of leading your brothers and sisters in this world. After I die, you must go on and teach them the old ways. You must keep our Irish tradition alive. Cherish the love you have for them and forget what you think you feel for Jack MacGrath."

She lowered her head.

Jack's heart cracked, right in two.

Choosing him meant turning her back on her father, her packmates, and the life she'd built in Ireland. If she chose to be with him, he'd be the happiest man in the world and elongate his life to a thousand years. But she would be disappointing the only family she'd ever had. Even if he lived every day of his life to make her happy, there would be a hole he couldn't fill. A shame that would burrow deep in her heart. She would know she'd turned her back on her loved ones, and she'd come to resent him for that.

I can't do that to her.

He couldn't make her choose between a life with him over a life with her pack. He knew the right answer in his bones. To him, they belonged together.

But there was no right answer for Isabelle.

And making her choose would break her.

With a burning ache in his heart, Jack watched Isabelle kneel down and embrace her father. Tried to imagine her heart filled with love for him and her packmates.

Good-bye, Isabelle.

And then he strode out of the museum, accepting the fact that he'd be dead before the year was through. His death wasn't what mattered at all. It was Isabelle's happiness.

That's all that had ever mattered in the first place.

Chapter Nineteen

"Have you heard from her?" Branson asked as they took their seat at the back of McDougal's Auction House.

Nodding, Jack eyed the front, where pieces were moving in and out. "She called right after I left Ireland. She left a message, asking me to call her back."

"Nothing since?" Branson waited for Jack to answer, and when he didn't, he said, "What'd she say? Have you listened to it yet?"

"No. I can't." Jack's hands shook, so he tucked them beneath his legs. "I fear listening to her voice would weaken my resolve."

"You know," Branson said, leaning closer, "for someone who held on so tight to something for so long, I didn't believe you'd give up the fight. You'd been searching for your Luminary for years. To give her up like that…I didn't expect it. Least of all from you."

"I didn't give up, Branson." He paused, remembering

how torn she'd looked in the museum that night. "I let her go. There's a big difference."

His friend nodded as if he understood, though he couldn't possibly. The pain he'd felt every single day had nearly killed him. Being away from Isabelle was torturous. At first, when he returned to San Francisco, Jack thought he might've been able to handle the separation as long as he focused on the time they had together. But that only made things worse. Now, Isabelle was on his mind twenty-four hours a day, and he constantly felt on the verge of a breakdown.

"I didn't think she'd send back the paintings," Branson blabbered on. "Not after you told her to keep them."

"Branson?" Jack glared. "Do you feel compelled to torture me today?"

"No sir," he said, smiling smugly. "I just can't wrap my mind around the fact that you're not together. You won't last long without—"

He stopped at Jack's sideways glance.

"Forgive me, sir. I shouldn't have overstepped."

"Nothing to forgive," Jack said. "You were merely stating the obvious. I'm getting weaker by the day. I thought I'd last the year, but after the toll this last month has taken on me, I'm not so sure."

It seemed that missing Isabelle had affected him more than he'd initially realized. He was used to feeling physically drained, but he hadn't expected heartbreak to be so damn exhausting. His shakes had gone from intermittent to near-constant, and when his headaches came on, they felt like chisels drilling into his temples. Blackouts were more common. With each one, he wondered whether it was going to be the last. One of these times, he simply wasn't going to come around at all.

"I thought the adrenaline kick from the skydiving would've held you over for a week."

"Ugh, don't remind me." Jack gave a hard shudder from the mere thought of it. "I'll take fifty shots in the leg before I'll jump out of a perfectly good airplane again."

As Colin announced a Monet, Jack's attention shifted to the front. Branson flipped through the brochure showing the day's art for auction.

"Did you find out which Bella Nolan piece is going up today?" Branson asked.

"Nothing more than it states in the brochure." Jack shook his head. "All it says is an exclusive piece. Never before seen. Isabelle sent back the pieces she borrowed after I returned to the city, so I'm not sure which one they have."

Which was precisely the reason he came today. Isabelle seemed to believe she had her entire collection showcased for her father. Either this was one she'd forgotten about, or a forgery.

He was here to find out which.

"Next up," Colin announced from the front, "we have a special Bella Nolan piece. It's *Werewolf in Dublin*, and never before seen."

Wait…*Werewolf in Dublin*?

He'd heard Isabelle mention that before…

Anticipation rattled in Jack's gut as the cloth was removed from the art, and Isabelle's words came back to him: *My first painting,* Werewolf in Dublin, *was of my father in wolf form, standing in front of Saint Patrick's Cathedral…he destroyed it.*

"Can't be…"

Sliding to the edge of his seat, Jack covered his hand with his mouth. Analyzed everything from the strokes and colors to the pressure of the brush and the signature on the bottom corner of the art.

"Unbelievable," he breathed.

The art was exactly how she'd described it. The spires of Saint Patrick's Cathedral rose up behind a gigantic black-haired wolf. The sky was dark and lumbering with clouds. Regal and robust, the wolf stood proud in front of the cathedral, though there was pain in his shadowed gaze.

The painting wasn't a forgery, which meant her father hadn't destroyed the painting after all. Then where had it been all these years? And how did Isabelle not know it existed?

Isabelle's words struck him: *It was drawn from a memory... at my mother's funeral.*

The fear and agony in the wolf's eyes gripped him. In the painting, her father had just lost his fated mate, the only woman in the world for him. Jack could relate. Wholeheartedly.

"Nothing will stop me from getting that painting," he whispered to Branson. "Nothing."

"We'll start the bidding at two and a quarter," Colin announced.

Jack flipped his paddle quickly, but the bid rose just as fast as someone in the front matched his bid, and then outdid it.

Colin's gaze skimmed the room. "Do we have three million?"

Jack lifted his hand.

"Sir," Branson said, tugging on his suit sleeve.

"Not now, Branson. Not a single distraction."

"But sir—"

"I said not now." Jack raised his paddle again as the bid soared near four million. "This is the most important piece I've ever acquired. Nothing will—"

"Sir, it's *her.*" He pointed to the front. "Look."

Rising off his seat, Jack searched the room, his gaze locking on the bidder in the front row. He could only see the back of her head, but he knew it was Isabelle. Dark locks of hair cascaded down her back and fell over her dainty shoulders. She flicked her wrist to bid again.

His heartbeat thrummed in his ears. His skin went flush. Breathing....*labored.*

He raised his paddle to outbid her and then scooted out from the back row. Everything zoomed far out as he made his way to the front. The auction might not have been happening at all. Voices were muffled, and the floor disappeared beneath his feet.

Up until this moment, he hadn't wanted to talk to her. Hadn't wanted to see her and rehash why they couldn't be together. Why he had to die for her to be happy.

But now that she was so close, he couldn't stop himself from going to her side.

He slid into the empty seat next to her, absentmindedly raising his paddle to counter her bid. As her gaze caught his, she stiffened in her seat and nervously flipped her hair over her shoulder.

"What are you doing here?" she said.

"I'm here for you." No, damn it. Scratch that. "For the painting," he spit out. "I heard there was a Bella Nolan piece, and I had to come."

"I…" She stopped what she'd been about to say, raised her paddle slowly as the bid raised to God-knew-what, and studied him carefully. "I thought about ringing you when I came into town, but after what happened, the way you just stopped talking to me…"

He countered her bid.

"…I didn't know what to say." She raised her paddle in defiance.

God, did she know how badly he wanted to take her hand? How much he wanted to hold her, if only for a second? But what would that help?

Nothing. It'd only make leaving her worse.

"How long are you in for?" he found himself asking.

She licked her lips slowly and let her tongue linger in the corner. Did she know what that did to him?

"Just for the day," she said.

They could do a lot in a day…

"Going once," Colin declared from the stage. "Sir?"

Jack dragged his attention to the painting. And raised his paddle again.

"I tried to call you," she whispered. Had her lips always been that delectable? Soft and pink, her lower lip slightly larger than the top. "I'm not sure if you got my message."

"I got it, but didn't listen to it."

She nodded, lowering her gaze to her lap. "Then you didn't hear that my father passed away."

"That's why you called?"

She nodded. "One of the reasons."

"I'm so sorry, Isabelle." As sadness gouged him, he took her hand and squeezed. Those same telling currents ran over his skin, warming him through. "I should've listened to it. I could've been there for you."

"There was nothing you could've done. He passed right after I showed him the exhibit. He enjoyed my art in his final moments, and we shared something special together. I revealed a side of myself that I'd kept hidden from him for so long. It meant the world to me that I was able to do that. And I was there at the end, which meant the world to him." She looked up at him, blinking through tear-heavy lashes. And ripped his heart clean out of his chest. "We said everything we'd always wanted to say but never could…everything except the one thing I wanted to hear most."

She didn't need to say what that was.

Her father hadn't given his blessing for them to be together.

He took back his hand. For her sake.

"Jack—"

"Sold!" Colin announced, cutting her short. "To Mr. MacGrath for eleven million."

Wow. Eleven.

He would've paid triple.

"Well, congratulations," she said, standing. "It'll be the perfect addition to your collection."

. . .

"Wait." His voice was soft and deep, a loving caress against her ears. Grabbing her by the elbow, he touched her gently. A reminder of the pull he had over her. "Isabelle."

She stopped, but couldn't meet his eye. "What?"

"Look at me."

God, she couldn't. Every second at his side was a testament to the strength of her will. She yearned to throw herself into his arms. To look into his eyes and see their future: a bonding ceremony, children, a home in the castle in Ireland. But those things would never be. Especially not now that her father had died without giving his blessing.

She had to put space between them. Be clearheaded about this whole thing the way she hadn't been before when she'd gotten lost in their connection, in their heat, and gone to bed with him.

Exhaling heavily, she turned and opened her eyes. "What do you want?"

His gaze bore into hers. "You have to know…"

She couldn't take much more of this. "I'm sorry, I can't."

"That's exactly why it had to end the way it did."

She felt her face frown. "Wait, did you—"

"Ms. Connelly?" Colin's crackly voice rang out, stopping her. "May I speak with you a moment?"

"Now's probably not the best time, Colin. May I call you when I'm on the road?"

"I'm sorry, but I'm afraid this can't wait." He wrung his hands in front of him. "This concerns you and Mr. MacGrath. Since you both happen to be here together, it appears now would be the best time."

As they followed him behind the stage, Jack said, "Is this about the painting?"

"Aye." Colin removed *Werewolf in Dublin* from its stand and brought it into a back room with them. "It is."

She eyed the painting as he handed it to Jack. Its beauty struck her even now. The colors were vibrant and crisp, her father's pain visceral as he stood in front of the cathedral.

"It looks exactly as I remember it," she said, stroking her hand over the top edge. "What's wrong?"

Jack eyed the back. Frowning, he pulled off an envelope and held it up.

"This was stapled to the frame," he said. "It has my name on the front."

Her breathing quickened. "What is it?"

Colin put up his hands, as if he was an innocent bystander in some elaborate heist. "The painting arrived here weeks ago with explicit orders to have the auction today, and the envelope was ordered to be sold with the painting. Other than that, I don't have a clue what it's about."

"Who would give instructions to have it sold today, specifically?" she thought aloud, and then turned her attention to Jack.

He tore through the top, pulled out a piece of paper, and skimmed to the bottom. "It's from your father."

"My—but how could he?" She felt the blood drain from her face. "Will you read it aloud?"

"My dearest Isabelle, I trust that Colin informed the proper people to get you and Jack to the auction house today, and I thank him dearly for that. I'm glad you were able to share your love of painting with me before I passed on. When you first gave this painting to me, I thought it was your way of saying you were turning away from the pack. Please forgive me for jumping to conclusions and ignoring your passion when you tried to present it to me. Though even in my anger, I couldn't destroy the piece. It was too beautiful and too perfect, much like you. After behaving so badly, I didn't know how to tell you I'd kept it. So I cherished it in solitude and kept it locked away. Until now."

She swallowed back a flood of tears as Jack read on.

"Jack, when I told you before that I'd never met a MacGrath who put another's happiness before his own, I wasn't lying. But now, I can honestly say that I know one who is good and decent, and loves my daughter wholeheartedly." Jack's reading pace slowed as his eyes tracked disbelievingly over the words. "The night you came to the museum to declare your love for my daughter—"

"You came?" she interrupted, her skin chilling. "To Ireland? The museum?"

He nodded without answering, and read on. "I knew you were there. I saw you hesitate, and ultimately decide that it was better for Isabelle to make her own path, to lead the pack, and to earn my respect. Well, Jack MacGrath, you have mine. Any man who would put his woman's happiness above his own life is a good man—one deserving of a father's blessing."

Even though Jack had read the words loud and clear, Isabelle couldn't wrap her head around what her father had said. Jack had come to see her, to fight for her, and then left? He'd seen the display? And then walked away so she could make her father proud?

He'd left so she wouldn't have to make the impossible choice…

"Jack…"

"There's more," he said, his voice full of sorrow. "This painting has always been one of my most treasured possessions. And I have cherished my daughter from the first day I held her in my arms. Now, I entrust them both to you, son. Take good care of them."

"Oh…God." She couldn't breathe. "I can't believe it."

Folding up the paper slowly, Jack replaced it in the envelope. "But how could he have been sure we'd be here, and that one of us would be the final bid out of everyone in the auction hall?"

Isabelle's gaze snapped to Colin. He winked and then backed out of the room, shutting the door behind him.

"You came to Dublin," she said, stepping closer. "You were in the museum that night…why didn't you tell me? Why didn't you say something?"

Jack leaned the painting against the wall. "Your father and I know why. And that's all that matters."

"And you got to talk to him?" She brushed her hand along the stubble on his jaw and then cupped his cheek in her hand. "It wasn't at the museum, so it had to have been beforehand. At the castle?"

He nodded.

"Then you saw my home," she said, warming from the inside out.

A smirk pulled at his lips. "Guess you could say I was given the extensive tour of the castle. From the ground up."

Frowning, she smoothed the stress lines as they appeared around his eyes. "Whatever that means."

Coiling his arms around her back, Jack tugged her against him. This was where she belonged, and wanted to be until the day she died.

"The most important thing is that your father gave us his blessing." Jack held her tight and nuzzled into her neck. His breath was warm and sweet and perfect as it blew into her hair. "We can finally be together…if you'll have me."

"Oh, Jack." She rose up on tiptoe and stamped her mouth to his, kissing him with every ounce of promise in her body. "Nothing would make me happier than being your wife and your bonded mate."

"I love you so much, Isabelle." Stroking his hands up and down her back, Jack squeezed her against him. Until they couldn't be closer without being one. "It was painful being away from you. I was physically ill…but nothing compared to the hole carved in my heart. You took a piece of me with you when you left."

"I know what you mean," she said, brushing her lips against his. "I left a piece of my heart behind with you in San Francisco. In your arms is the only place I feel whole."

He rested his forehead against hers and breathed in deeply. "I'm suddenly dizzy."

"What's the matter?" she asked, pulling back to get a good look at him. He was pale. "Is it a lack of adrenaline?"

"No, it's you." He tipped her chin up with his fingers and then kissed her, making the world and everything else around them disappear. "If I said you strengthen me and weaken me at the same time, would you understand what I mean?"

She shook her head. "Not really. But if you take me home, you can explain it to me all night long."

"And tomorrow, too," he promised, kissing the tip of her nose. "And the next day, and the one after that."

"I love you, Jack." Her heart beat strong and true. "Always."

"Come on," he said, tucking her under one arm and the painting under the other. "Let's go home."

"Which home will that be?"

"Ireland, of course. Your place is there, ruling over the pack. And my place is with you."

He was a great man. It was a good thing her father got to see that before he passed.

"That sounds wonderful," she said, heart fluttering with excitement. "But would you mind if we stopped by your place first? There's something I want to show you."

He glanced down at her. "At my place?"

She nodded. "A little surprise. I had it delivered this morning. I tried to catch you there, but apparently you'd already left for the auction."

"You never cease to amaze me."

Wait until he saw what was in his driveway…

Chapter Twenty

"I told you I'd replace it."

"You've *got* to be kidding me." Turning into his driveway, Jack stared at the massive marble fountain that'd replaced his last one. "Is that...Aphrodite?"

Isabelle nodded excitedly and leaned over him to point out the driver's-side window. "She's bathing."

"She's naked."

"Is that all you see?" She smacked him playfully in the shoulder. "She's graceful and elegant, and so much classier than your last one."

"I agree with you there," he said, shrugging, "but did you have to buy one so...big? Look at her. She's massive. Over eight feet tall, at least."

"Yes, but she's also the goddess of love. She deserves to be the focal point of your yard. Besides, this place could use a woman's touch."

He gave a groan as he took her hand and placed it over his heart. "Speaking of needing your touch..."

Heat sparked through his palm and splintered into his

chest as she rested her head on the seat back and nailed him with a lustful stare. And then, tantalizingly slow, he moved her hand lower, down his abs, to the ridge of his slacks. She sat perfectly still, her gaze raking up and down his body, drinking him in.

Leaning over, he closed her mouth over hers, gently grazing his teeth against her lower lip. She mewed in response and slid her hands around his neck. Urging him on. He wanted to taste more of her, all of her, right here in this car.

"We should get inside," he said, and nearly leaped out of the car.

The second he met her around the other side, he dragged her against him and closed his mouth over hers. Guiding her back, back, back, he held her tight as he stepped up the stairs and pushed through the doorway of his home. Branson had taken her car from the museum, parked it in his garage, and left the door open for them. Jack had told his friend to "take a walk," which meant he and Isabelle had the place to themselves for the night.

Which is exactly what he needed.

By the time the night was through, Isabelle would be screaming his name.

She would be *his,* body and soul, forever.

Kicking the door closed, Jack pinned Isabelle against the wall with his hips and held her hands over her head. Possessing her mouth, he tangled his tongue with hers and explored the deep, wet recess of her mouth. The primal urge to claim her, here and now, fluttered through him and then caught.

"We should get upstairs," he said between ravenous kisses. He skimmed a hand down her lean body, stopping over the flat span at her belly button, and then gripped her hip. "Before I take you against the wall. This wasn't the romantic encounter I'd envisioned for tonight."

She grinned against his mouth. "You had no idea I was

coming. How could you have planned something romantic?"

Now it was his turn to smirk. Using two fingers against her chin, he directed her attention to the stairs. He'd had hundreds of red and white rose petals laid out. Candles flickered from every stair, winding up to the second floor. It was as romantic as he could arrange in the brief thirty-minute drive from the auction hall to his front door.

"Wow." She dropped her hands to her sides. "It's…magic."

Actually, Branson had set it up.

"I'm glad you like it."

"I do, I love it. But I wasn't talking about the roses." She spun back into his arms. "*You* are pure magic."

He smudged kisses down the silky-smooth curve of her neck. "Me?"

"What you do to me." Leaning her head back against the wall, Isabelle panted for air. "You melt me, Jack. One kiss and I can't breathe."

On command, he brushed his lips against hers, and then plunged his tongue into her mouth. She moaned, a soft, seductive sound that tested his control.

As he let her up for air, she said, "One touch and I'm quivering."

He cupped her breasts, cradling their heavy weight in his hands. Beneath her shirt, her nipples beaded, responding to his touch. And then she shook. Trembled against him.

"If you don't take me now," she said, beginning to writhe against him, "I may come apart fully clothed."

"That would be a damn shame."

Going easy, as slow as he could with his waning restraint, he bunched the fabric of her shirt in his fists and then guided it off her glorious body. Her lusciously full breasts overflowed from a dainty silk-and-lace bra. On a throaty moan, his knees buckled and he knelt before his queen.

"You've got unbelievable breasts," he said, stroking his

hands over her curves. "Soft and smooth." Easing down her bra, he revealed perfectly pink nipples, hardened from arousal. He rolled one with his tongue and kneaded her other breast with his hand. "You're exquisite. Every inch of you."

She dug her fingers through his hair and then clawed at his shoulders as he buried his face between her breasts.

Her caress lit something in him. A hunger that couldn't be satiated from mere touch alone. He went tight, head to toe, as if a lightning rod speared through him. Sensations balled at the base of his spine as she arched against the wall and lifted her hips toward him. The scent of her arousal—fragrant and sweet—hit him, nearly knocking him off his feet.

His self-control was fading fast.

As a growl erupted from his chest and he reached around to grab her backside, Isabelle's eyes went wide. But shock didn't light those amazing green depths. It was lust and ravenous thirst.

It fueled him on.

Jack stood and crushed his mouth to hers. Lifted her off her feet and cradled her in his arms. She squealed as her feet kicked out, but quickly melted into his arms. He made it halfway up the stairs before the second dizzy spell of the night struck him.

He set her down carefully, leaned against the banister, and rubbed his forehead. Stars danced in front of his eyes. His stomach tumbled. And something in his chest tugged.

"Are you okay?" she asked, coming into his line of sight. "Jack?"

"I'm fine. Bring those lips back here again."

And she did, pouncing on him with more force than he realized she had. She nipped and bit, licking one corner of his mouth before sliding her tongue along his. She seized him full-bodied, her hands wrapped around his neck, her breasts pressed against his chest, her mouth slanting along his.

A lick of heat scorched through him as blinding light flashed before his eyes.

Fisting two sides of his dress shirt, he jerked, tearing it down the center. Buttons flew, rolling down the stairs.

"Get out of your pants," she ordered.

He quirked an eyebrow. "Only if you do the same."

Her lips curled in approval as she kicked off her shoes and stepped out of her pants. Matching lace panties—white as snow, soft as silk—begged for his touch.

"Good Lord, Isabelle." After removing his shoes, he yanked down his pants, but it wasn't fast enough. Nothing would be fast enough. "You're a goddess."

His mouth was already watering, anticipating the sweet taste of her succulent flesh. But seeing those panties…it nearly broke him.

Urging her down onto the stairs, she stretched out for him, gripping the banister rail for support. He spread her legs wide. Moved aside her panties and licked a long, slow line through her heat.

He groaned.

Her thighs shivered around his head in answer.

"Jack…" She gazed at him down her body, through her breasts, between her legs. Her gaze was hot and heavy-lidded. Desirous. "After the last time we were together, I was the one supposed to be pleasuring you tonight."

"Oh, believe me." Another long lap of his tongue. Another jerking shudder. "The pleasure is mine."

He put his mouth on her until she shook uncontrollably. Until the banister rail cracked and her hips bucked against his mouth. He kissed her intimately, flicking her clit, sucking and humming in appreciation as he drew the orgasm closer. Her hips began to move against his mouth, back and forth, back and forth. And when he dived his tongue inside her, she reared up, tugging at his shoulders.

"Oh God, Jack, I'm so close—" She panted, fighting for air. "I need you inside me. *Please*."

Rising to his feet, Jack swept her into his arms and carried her into his bedroom, where he laid her on the bed. She scooted back, eyeing him with dark desire in her eyes. As he crawled on top of her, a migraine slammed into him.

Hammer to the forehead.

Knives to the temples.

He rested over her, his hips between hers, his erection against her leg.

Breathe.

Just breathe.

"Jack?" Her angelic voice floated to him from somewhere far away. "Jack, can you hear me?"

The strumming sound of her heartbeat resonated against his, recharging the energy stirring in his veins. "Believe me, love. I'm fine."

"Good." She glided her hands up and down the muscles on his back as she coiled her legs around his waist. "Because I'm nowhere near through with you yet."

His lips crashed against hers as he fell on top of her. Swirling his tongue in her mouth, against her cheek, over her lower lip, he positioned himself close to her heat. And then, with a full-body shudder, he thrust himself inside her.

As their hips met, they groaned in unison. Isabelle dropped her head back and arched up, thrusting her breasts against his chest.

"Yes," she hissed through clenched teeth. "Just like that."

He slid out and in again. Slowly. Massaging her depths. Filling her completely. And when their hips met again, her mouth dropped open in a sultry O. Bracing himself on his arms, he plunged his tongue into her mouth, tasting her sweetness. Bathed in her warmth.

Mine.

"I'm yours," she mouthed against him. As if she'd heard the voice inside him. "Always."

His heart stuttered, though his hips seemed to know their rhythm by memory. Blood rushed to his ears. He buried himself deep—God, so deep—inside her, until he was drowning in her scent and her warmth.

"Will you have me?" He drove inside her as his words broke. "As your mate?"

She nodded, her dark hair fanning out beneath her. "Of course I will."

"You have no idea what that means to me, my Bella."

As tenderly as he could, he pinned her to the mattress, entwining his fingers with hers. As their palms met, he sank his thick length deep. She moaned in satisfaction, the breath punching out of her and fanning over his face.

"Palm to palm," he said, sliding out of her core. "Heart to heart." The rock in his chest thudded, slower now. "From this moment on, we shall never part."

They were the spoken bonds one Luminary makes to another. When their bodies, their hearts, and their souls could join as one. He'd dreamed of speaking these vows to Isabelle, though he couldn't have dreamed it would've been as good, as perfect, as this.

She was everything to him. A friend, a lover, and now, his true soul mate.

As he leaned down to kiss her and show her the depth of his love, darkness zoomed in around him. There simply wasn't air to fill his lungs. He wanted to tell Isabelle to hurry, to speak the words before they lost the chance. But he couldn't rush her, not even now.

Her loving gaze held his. "Palm to palm, heart to heart." She rocked her hips beneath him, so that he eased inside her. "From this moment on, we shall never part."

Finally.

As sweet, sweet relief soared through him, starbursts of brilliant white-hot energy snaked through his body, filling him with more light and warmth than he could contain. Unadulterated love and happiness burst through him, radiating through his skin and into Isabelle. In his mind's eye, his soul shattered, burst through his skin, and melded with hers.

"You're mine," she whimpered, her core pulsing around him. She clutched at his shoulders, bringing him down over her. "I'm yours."

He pressed himself against her, skin against skin, mouth to mouth. "Forever, and a day."

When he opened his eyes, through the blinding light and the blissful pain, Isabelle's expression was pure ecstasy. Her mouth dropped open, robbed of breath. Her eyes rolled back. And her center clenched around his with unrelenting pulses. As she throbbed around him, milking his shaft harder and harder, he drove himself to the hilt, giving her everything.

Grasping at his shoulders, tight in the grip of the orgasm, she stared into his eyes. Right through to his soul. Cried out his name. Over and over again. It was a sound of passion, of desperate relief. And then it was reverent. A sobbing sound that ripped from her lips as another orgasm rolled through her.

This time, his muscles tensed with her. He quivered on the brink. And then, with a hard beat of his heart, he emptied himself into her.

A few minutes later, when he was resting over her body, still and lifeless, the air in his lungs finally returned.

"My Bella," he panted into her mane of dark, silky hair. "You've saved me."

"I know. I thought for a second I was going to lose you."

"It's more than that." His heartbeat drummed in his rib cage, stronger than he'd ever remembered it being, even in his youth. "I was dying on the inside, too. I didn't know I could love someone this much."

She squeezed him against her and sighed.

"I'd do anything for you, Isabelle." He kissed her shoulder. "Anything. All you have to do is the say the word, and I'll make it happen. Your happiness is my only regard from this moment forward. For as long as we both shall live."

"Are you sure about that?"

Her voice was playful, stirring something inside him.

"I'll rope you the moon if you want it," he said. "Just ask."

With lightning-quick werewolf speed, she flipped him over and pinned him to the mattress. Straddling his middle, she rolled her hips, bringing him to life once more.

"I want you to move back with me to Ireland," she commanded, a sly curl on the edges of her lips. "I want to have a big induction ceremony in front of the pack, where they'll welcome you in with open arms."

Even though he was exhausted beyond measure, he went hard beneath her. Curling his hands around her hips, he slipped into her heat and eased into a slow, sensual rhythm.

"Sounds like heaven." In his lustful haze, the words were staccato, but they were clear. "What else?"

"I want kids, too." With a soft groan, she arched back, giving him a stunning view of her breasts. "Lots and lots of crazy kids running around, shifting into werewolves at every full moon."

He tugged gently on her arm, bringing her down over the top of him. "Sweetheart, the picture you're painting right now sounds like a masterpiece."

She kissed him, softly, openmouthed, filling him with more love and life than he'd ever dreamed possible.

Acknowledgments

As always, thanks to the amazing team at Entangled Publishing for believing in the Seattle and San Francisco Wolf Pack books: Liz Pelletier, Candace Havens, Katie Clapsadl, and Curtis Svehlak, a few treasures among many.

Thanks to my agent, Nalini Akolekar, for leading the charge.

I'm so beyond blessed to have the best team of friends, readers, plotters, critiquers, supporters, cheerleaders, and lovable crazies at my side: Elisa Dane, Virna DePaul, Susan Hatler, Vanessa Kier, Jennie Marts, Laurie Shaw, Monica Wunderlich, and Lora Walker. Special thanks to Aggie Smith for pulling through with last-minute reads and honest feedback. (Those brutally honest opinions are given with love and smiles, I know it.)

Hugs, love, and thanks to Justin, Kelli, and Gavin, and the rest of my family for the unwavering love and support.

About the Author

New York Times and USA Today best-selling author Kristin Miller writes sweet and sassy contemporary romance and paranormal romance of all varieties. Kristin has degrees in psychology, English, and education, and taught high school and middle school English before crossing over to a career in writing. She lives in Northern California with her alpha male husband and their two children. She loves chocolate way more than she should, and the gym less. You can usually find her in the corner of a coffee shop, laptop in front of her and mocha in hand, using the guests around her as fuel for her next book.

Facebook
Twitter
Web

Discover more paranormal romance titles from Entangled...

DRAKON'S PROMISE
a *Blood of the Drakon* novel by N.J. Walters

Darius Varkas is a drakon. He's neither human nor dragon. He's both. He and his brothers are also the targets of an ancient order who want to capture all drakons for their blood, which can prolong a human's life. When Sarah Anderson finds a rare book belonging to the Knights of the Dragon, she's quickly thrust into a dangerous world of secrets and shifters. And when the Knights realize Sarah has a secret of her own, she becomes just as much a target as Darius. Her scary dragon shifter just might be her best chance at survival.

FLYING THROUGH FIRE
a *Dark Desires* novel by Nina Croft

Thorne's willpower has been honed over ten thousand years. He might want Candy, but the last thing he needs is an infatuation with a young, impetuous werewolf. Candy makes him lose control, and that could have disastrous consequences. As the threat escalates and they become separated by time and space, Candy must find a way back to him, because while Thorne alone has the power to defeat the dragons, only together can they finally bring peace to the universe.

THE HUNT

a *Shifter Origins* novel by Harper A. Brooks

Prince Kael has just lost his father to an assassin, and he's the next target. A murderer is on the loose, the kingdom is in disarray, and Kael is determined to make the person responsible for killing his father pay. But falling for the beautiful Cara, panther-shifter assassin and main suspect his father's murder, wasn't part of the plan. He's not at all sure she did it, and he finds himself going against everything he's ever known just to claim her.

SON OF THUNDER

a novel by Libby Bishop

Rune is the grandson of Thor, and just as strong. Exiled to the realm of Earth for nearly killing his brother–it was a little misunderstanding– he has to find a way to redeem himself so he can get back to Asgard. And when he lands—literally—in the bed of a fiery redhead with an FBI badge, he realizes that she may be the key to going home. But helping Liv hunt a killer has one big consequence—chemistry. He can't keep his hands off her, and there's no way they can ever be together.